Neurophysiology
&
the Human Heart

ALICIA V MCCLANE

ISBN: 9781718077874

Cover design by: Alicia V McClane using Canva (Raleway, Garet and Glacial Indifference fonts). Novel printed using PT Serif font.

Thank you, Joe, Lauren, Becky, and Alex, for your generous feedback and enthusiasm.

1

The app politely informs me that I have reached my destination; I flick off autopilot and glance up at the dull, boarded-up shop. Not quite what I had envisioned when Riya had described her experience. I thumb back to the email on my phone and pick out the address again. The street and unit number matches, but surely this cannot be a lab.

"Nic!" I startle hearing my name and look up to see Riya waving as she approaches from the brighter end of the street. I meet her half way and she leans in for a brief hug.

"Bloody hell you're twitchy!" she laughs.

"Is there a relaxed way to loiter in an alleyway?" my voice comes out unpleasantly thin, "I was just about to call you-"

"What? I'm not even late," Riya taps her watch to reveal the time. "Bang on seven."

"Yeah, I just thought I was in the wrong place," I say, trying to clear some of the tension in my throat. "So where are we going?"

Riya hooks her arm through mine and leads me back down the alleyway. Her other arm cradles a thick ream of paper.

"I'm playing along." She pre-empts my question and nods to a faded sign above one of the shuttered shops. It reads *Ryan's Bookbinding*. Riya leans in to its battered door and buzzes the intercom. A distant bell sounds, then fades to a hum and a woman's voice crackles:

"Sorry, we're closed."

I glance at Riya, who is still smiling.

She leans in towards the machine, "Hello, it's Riya - we spoke earlier. I've got an urgent drop-off." Her voice is cool, but she is squeezing my arm.

"I'll buzz you in," the voice replies.

"Wait, we're going in here?" I ask, my pulse thrumming suddenly.

Riya grins and drops my arm to push open the door. Behind is an unlit stairwell which she enters without hesitation. I follow, tamping down my unease with a mental reminder that Riya has been here before. At the top of the stairs, Riya turns left into a bright room. I slip in behind her and scan the space. It looks more like a doctor's reception than a lab. The room is sparse, just a few items of plain furniture; a desk, computer, coffee table and a narrow, grey sofa. No magazines or flyers on the table, or posters on the walls. A door beside the reception desk opens and a short, blonde woman enters. Her muted grey dress matches the interior.

"Good evening, Riya," the woman says, sidling behind the desk and tapping into the computer. "Who is your friend?" There is rigidity in her voice and blood rushes to my face. I had assumed my attendance was agreed ahead of time.

"This is my friend Nicole, from work," Riya appears oblivious to the tone. "Last time I came I mentioned that the project might interest her. She's a fellow Psychologist at the University," Riya turns to me. "And this is Ellen, she's the creator-"

"Script writer," Ellen interrupts. "Professor McAllister created the program."

"Oh yes, sorry I get confused because you *create* the scenarios."

As Riya rambles on with her justification, Ellen shifts her pale eyes towards me, locking on with an unsettling intensity. I turn back to Riya, trying to think of an easy way to bail.

"So yeah, I invited Nicole along because I think she'd appreciate the lab." Riya rounds off her spiel. "She works in cognitive research so this project is right up her street."

Riya winks at me, seemingly unaware of the awkward atmosphere she has created. I start mentally spinning an escape plan, but Ellen cuts in:

"It might be useful to get your feedback actually. The program is in beta so we're still smoothing out bugs. That's why it is invite only."

There is stiffness at the end of the sentence, but Ellen's face remains impassive. After some quick typing, a nearby printer starts spouting sheets which she collects and affixes to a clipboard.

"All set," Ellen switches to a well-practiced smile. "Would you two like to follow me?"

Riya looks at me and jerks her shoulder up in a gesture that says *why not*? I try to shake off the awkwardness of the reception and follow them through to the adjoining room. Dim lights come on automatically to reveal a disappointingly bland set up; a small space housing an array of computers, wires and several office chairs on wheels. A window replaces the top half of the far wall looking onto a large, empty room. Ellen sets about flicking switches and pressing various buttons, then four monitors beneath the glass light up with activity.

"Voilà, the Vie Lab," she says with little ceremony.

There are a couple of chairs positioned in front of the computer screens, and Ellen gestures for me to sit. She slides over a sheet of paper and a pen saying, "Could you sign this non-disclosure form please?" I scan the technical wording and am reminded of debriefing forms we give to participants after psychology experiments. I sign away my right to discuss the project in public.

"Riya, would you like to leave your things here - if you're ready to start?" Ellen says, sitting down next to me.

Riya places the stack of papers she is clutching onto a chair, sheds her jacket and handbag and heaps them on top. She is now down to a fitted, blue dress and nude flats. After a slow exhale she says "Ready," and stands next to the door. Whilst she waits for the signal to enter, she rolls her long, black hair up in a bun, and her face looks nervous for the first time, an unfamiliar flicker in her expression. I smile at her, trying to look enthusiastic, but unease rises in my chest.

"Please go on through," Ellen says to Riya without taking her eyes from the computer where she is operating various coding terminals. I shuffle my chair closer to the window to watch Riya enter the empty room and drift towards the centre. Her posture is more cramped up than usual, one hand up near her face twisting loose hair.

Ellen leans over to speak into a desktop mic.

"Can you hear me, Riya?"

"Yes!" Riya says, waving in our direction.

"She can't see us, it's one-way glass," Ellen says flatly before turning back to the mic. "Riya, we're about to start. Remember that to exit at any time say, *end game* - OK?" Riya nods. "Great, initiating programme now. The lights will drop, this is normal to reboot the system."

Ellen releases the microphone and taps at her keyboard again. A series of symbols appear on the leftmost screen, and at once the lights in Riya's room go out. The lights also dim in the control room.

"Oh, put this on," Ellen says, pressing a black metal hoop into my hands. "Align the red bar with the centre of your forehead like this," she lifts her own band and places it like a narrow crown on her head. "It allows you to visualise the room we generate." I do as I am told, trying to figure out how this flimsy machinery functions as virtual reality equipment.

Ellen mumbles to herself whilst typing out a series of numbers from the clipboard in front of her. I watch her complete the task, confirming a few messages on the screen and sitting back to observe the outcome. The lights in the other room flicker back on, but to my surprise, the empty room now resembles a doctor's office, with an examination table, drawers and trollies of medical equipment. Everything looks straight out of a medical drama, even down to anatomy posters on the walls. I let out an involuntary gasp, and Ellen glances sideways at me, her eyes crinkles a little.

"Hold on to your hat," she says.

My eyes are wide open, trying to comprehend how I am seeing this, tempted to lift off the headband like 3D glasses at the cinema to check that the plain room hasn't changed somehow, but I don't want to break the illusion.

Riya is beside herself inside the room, awkwardly crossing and uncrossing her arms. A loud knocking jolts her still. To her left, a door opens, and a man enters. The man looks remarkably like Leo Kissenger, a 90s-era heartthrob from the medical drama *Dial Triple Nine*.

I break away from my rigid observation to whisper to Ellen, "Is that Leo Kissenger?"

"Well, it's Riya's mental image of Leo Kissenger," Ellen mutters back without taking her eyes off her screen. I find this hard to comprehend, how can I see *her image* of him?

The doc scans a clipboard and says "Riya Cooper?" his voice rich and familiar, straight out of an advert. "Here for a routine check-up?" Riya nods, beaming.

Though it feels like talking in the cinema, I have to ask, "Did Riya specifically ask for him in an hospital scene?"

The silhouette of Ellen's head nods in the dark.

"Aren't these more like nightmare scenarios?" I press.

Ellen laughs through her nose, "Worst nightmare for some people, sexual fantasy for others. You'd be surprised how often the two overlap."

My blood runs cold. Sexual fantasy? Was I about to watch my friend live out some exhibitionist sex dream? No wonder Riya didn't tell me any details. My attention snaps back to the white room, and I wonder whether it is too late to leave politely. But curiosity weighs in with shock and I stay fixed in my seat, watching.

"If you could please remove your dress and take a seat on the examination bench, I'll be with you in a second," Doc

Kissenger says, drawing a blue curtain around the table to give Riya some privacy.

It crosses my mind that this could be an elaborate joke; Riya loves to make out that I am a prude. I look to Ellen, wondering whether to call her out, but see that she is hunched over the keyboard, immersed in the code. I hear the curtains open, and my stomach tightens.

Riya is sitting upright wearing only her underwear. Very small lace knickers and a thin veil of a bra covering her modest breasts. I shuffle in my chair.

"OK," Kissenger speaks, eerily familiar, "if you'd like to lie back, I'm going to check a few vitals."

He lifts his hand to her throat and uses two fingers to count the beat of the pulse in her neck. His face remains unchanged as his hand the slides to her neck, then collar bone. He runs a couple of fingers underneath her bra, over her nipples. Riya sucks in a sharp breath and he pauses, looks to her face, then slips her bra straps from her shoulders. Now her breasts are released from their lace coverings, he appears to lose interest and picks up his clipboard to make a quick note.

"Perfect. Now I need to check your heart rate."

He removes the stethoscope from around his neck and presses the end to her now bare left breast. He glances to his watch to count the beats. Riya is chewing her lower lip, trying to control her grin.

"OK, now some slow breaths in and out." Riya obliges.

I notice the doctor's free hand returned to her body, sliding down towards her right thigh and settling at the edge of her knickers. Riya's legs tense as his fingers slip beneath the fabric.

All the while his other hand casually holds the stethoscope to her chest.

Riya's face is flushed, and mine burns too. I side-glance at Ellen, who is busy studying the screen in front of her, leaning in closely. I find her disassociation from the situation in the white room intriguing. She seems almost oblivious to it, her thoughts elsewhere processing numbers and letters.

When I face the room again, Riya had started to arch her back to the doctor's touch. He appears to be concentrating, the right-hand job a background task. Riya lets out her first gasp of pleasure just as the doctor withdraws his hand and picks up his pen to note something. Riya snaps open her eyes, the disappointed expression on her face almost comical.

Ellen glances briefly from her screen to the room, then back to her work, typing a few notes into a terminal. Meanwhile, Kissenger pulls a small silver torch from his shirt pocket and clicks the end.

"I'm going to have a quick look in your ears now," he says, stepping closer to the bed. She sits and he gently pulls the lobe of her left ear and shines a light into the canal. Their bodies are almost touching.

"Perfect, and the right," he takes a step to the right of her, again with a fraction of space between them. This time, as he leans in to examine her ear, there is a subtle shift in his stance and his leg presses lightly against her thigh. He switches off the light without a word, places it back into his pocket, and repositions himself between her legs. In a swift movement, he pulls her closer, kissing her firmly on the lips, his hands around her hips. Riya shifts to facilitate the removal of underwear.

I don't realise my hands are at my face until I brush the headband with my fingers. The reality of the situation swims back. This isn't an erotic film; this is my friend and her imagination. The situation has a dreamy feel, like I couldn't wake if I wanted to.

I become aware of Ellen frantically typing something on the keyboard nearest to me. Her speed seems to be keeping pace with the action in the room. She switches between screens as the two in the room change position. The combination of hands and bodies quicken until there is a gasp of pleasure from the room, and I feel a spring of relief myself. Surely, it is nearly over.

When I look back to the room, the doc is hitching up his trousers.

"Everything seems to be working fine, I have no concerns. I'll give you a minute to get dressed and pop your file down to reception."

With that he draws the curtain around Riya, who is sitting looking quite bewildered, and exits through the internal door. The room is still.

Moments later, Riya emerges from behind the curtain, looking somewhat dishevelled, clears her throat and says, "end game."

Ellen leans over to speak into the microphone again. "That's great, thanks Riya. I'll drop the lights and you can exit when the door reappears."

The lights flicker off and on as Riya approaches the door. The room is empty again. Riya looks like she has just stepped off a rollercoaster, a mixture of confusion and ecstasy on her face. "Bloody hell, that was good!" she grins as she enters the

9

control room. No trace of embarrassment on her face; her statuesque posture regained.

Leo bloody Kissenger, she raises a palm to me, requesting a congratulatory high five. I give it to her; both of our hands are hot. The lights in the control room drop and we are ushered out.

2

Ellen leads us back through to the reception room where she files away my non-disclosure form. I linger for a second, debating whether to ask, as Riya beelines for the door.

"Do you need any more testers?" I say quickly, my voice high and tight.

Ellen looks at me blankly and I await the apology, a flush spreading across my neck. I hear Riya sigh, either in impatience or out of pity, it's hard to tell over the buzz in my ears.

"There is one free slot in a few weeks actually; a tester is on holiday," Ellen says without looking away from my face. "We could pencil you in as a one off if you'd like?"

The buzzing in my ears whirrs an octave higher and I nod keenly, Ellen's subsequent sentences blurring together. She slides over a piece of paper, and I write down my number, trying to make the digits stand up straight. In response, she notes the date and time of the appointment on a blank business card. I tuck it into the pocket of my jeans and smile, making a swift exit.

"Well, aren't you a jammy git," Riya jabs me in the ribs the second we leave the building. "I was told that each tester has to be approved by Professor McAllister based on professional merits. I guess it's not *what* you know, but *who* you know after all." I smirk, unable to conjure any witty comebacks.

As we walk up to where Riya's vintage Mini is parked, we whisper and giggle about some of the details from the scenario. Riya is as casual at discussing the intimacies as she is spilling details about guys she meets online. It's hard to comprehend that one was technically imaginary. The chat winds to a close when we reach Riya's car, parked a little too close to the adjacent car. Despite the confidentiality agreement fresh in my mind, I can't help but squeeze in one hushed question about the lab itself.

"So do they explain how it works?" I ask, my voice low.

Riya fiddles in her bag for her car keys, answering absently, "Sort of, but they don't give too much away because of intellectual property rights or something. Besides, I feel like knowing how it works would ruin the fun," she grins and opens the car door. "All they need from me is my trusty feedback."

She withdraws into her tiny car, making me smile as her long limbs tuck into the cramped driving seat. Sometimes this woman's obsession with style gets the better of her. She offers me a lift home, but I'd rather walk; it is a warm evening, and I enjoy the quiet hum of midweek Manchester. I also need to shift some excited tension before I get back to my quiet flat.

The walk home is swift as I burn through the energy of my own thoughts. I replay each segment of the night but fixate on the final exchange with Ellen. Had she given me the appointment reluctantly, out of pity? Would she get in trouble for booking someone who wasn't handpicked by the Professor? I cringe about it for a couple of streets, then push the thought away. No point dwelling on a situation when you achieved the ideal outcome. Sometimes psychology skills outplay self-consciousness.

By the time I get back to my flat, it is gone 9pm. I kick off my shoes and head straight to the kitchenette. Though I am too keyed up to be hungry, I reach for a cereal box out of habit. The final handful slides into the bowl with a trickle of crumbs. As I flatten the box down to add to the recycling, I see that there are already two other boxes of the same sugar flakes sat in there. Thinking back over the past few weeks, I realise that I've eaten cereal for dinner on multiple occasions; an embarrassing meal pattern for a comfortably employed, twenty-nine-year-old woman. I flip the box over and scan the nutrition panel; at least there are some added vitamins in there, so I am not on track for scurvy.

I take the cereal to the small wooden table near the window and prise my laptop open. As the system loads, I crunch through the flakes and look out of the window. Sadly, I am not in the high-level flats, which are extortionately priced compared to my modest studio, so there isn't much to see apart from red bricks and pigeons. But the quiet night-time scene is relaxing on the eyes.

My start-up programmes ping to life with a stream of notifications. I dismiss them all, and open a private internet browser, resisting the urge to rub my hands together as I prepare for a little internet stalking. If the Vie Lab was linked to the University, then there would be something about the project in the digital ether. I hover over the keyboard, digging

13

my teeth into my bottom lip, thinking. I know what I want to search, but running "Vie Lab," through a search engine seems unwise after those confidentiality forms. But surely researching *people* wouldn't raise any red flags, I could have met Ellen at a psychology conference, after all. Or a bar.

I expected to be able to pull up some sort of social profile using her first name, location and research topic. Instead, I find myself sifting through endless photos and bios of other people called Ellen. I need her surname. My fingers itch to message Riya and ask her whether she knows, but then I remember Professor McAllister. That is a more unusual name.

Sure enough, several keystrokes later I am looking at McAllister's online research profile. It is one of those auto-generated profiles using data captured by search engines. The page has pulled together a great list of published papers. I scan the titles, picking out neuroimaging terms that I am familiar with, and complex computer programming terms I am not. The last publication date was five years ago. Either the list is out of date, or McAllister swapped from research lab to Vie Lab several years ago.

There's a lingering curiosity steering me back to Ellen and I find myself scanning the list of authors wondering if any of them might be her. But, disappointingly, the names are cryptically listed with initials only. Then it dawns on me that Ellen might not even be a published researcher and the search loses momentum. Fatigue is creeping in, blurring the text on screen. Reluctantly, I put my laptop to sleep.

3

The Coffee Machine Cafe is normally rammed with students, but during the summer holidays there are only a handful of international students occupying the multi-coloured tables. Riya and I meet at the cafe once a week for lunch to catch up, and to get out of our respective research blocks. Working in different areas of psychology means we don't get to see each other day-to-day, and, without trying, we often evaded sunlight too. Riya is waiting by the entrance, scrolling through her phone. It is a little jarring to see her after last night; though we have been close friends for about four years, we've never been *that* close.

"I finally got a reply about that manuscript," she says, glancing briefly away from her screen to check it is me approaching. It was not the greeting I'd expected; I was fully prepared for coded chat about the Vie Lab. My mind is overspilling with questions. We shuffle into the short queue for food, and I browse the sandwiches whilst Riya flicks through her phone. I ask a few general questions about her research paper, but Riya isn't really listening.

"Sorry, I'll get off this in a second," she says. "I'm just a bit behind work after last night - I could not concentrate at *all* yesterday!" She pockets her phone and leans in to whisper. "And work is clearly not the best place to have these kinds of thoughts." I laugh, relieved that she wants to divulge.

I hurriedly pay for my baguette and Americano, then find a nice, secluded spot for us to sit by the window. Riya drops her bag next to mine and sits down.

"I love these summer specials!" she declares, digging into a colourful pasta salad. I exercise all my self-control to allow her to eat a few bites before launching into the chat I want to have:

"Honestly, I don't know how you were so blasé about last night–"

Riya nearly chokes to interrupt and shush me. She looks around, sees that no-one is sat nearby, then leans in dramatically.

"This isn't the place to talk about that Nicole!" she whispers. "Why do you think I've never discussed it here before?" This is a good point, Riya is a keen over-sharer, yet she has never let on any details from her first session.

Riya pushes back into her chair and continues to eat her salad. "Come around to mine tonight and we can unpick the scenario to your heart's content." My heart sinks at the prospect of waiting half of a tedious day to discuss, but I smile and nod. Riya leads the conversation for a while, and I listen whilst I eat. Eventually I am invested in her weekend date story.

"There's no playing-hard-to-get with this guy, which is refreshing." Riya says, "We just met for dinner in town, that new place with the one syllable name. What's it called?" she chews her salad, thinking. "Oh yeah, Coze!" She rolls her eyes. Manchester has cycled through so many new restaurants that the names seem to have become competitively absurd. "I had a few wines, and it was all very nice, so I suggested we skip dessert and head back to my place." Her eyebrows imply what she is excluding from the conversation. You can't be too careful sharing intimate details on campus, everyone at the University seems to be connected by a degree or two.

"You can tell me all about it tonight," I smile, but secretly wonder if I've already had enough intimate details about Riya to last me a lifetime.

"I mean, it was hardly *Kissenger* standard," she amuses herself saying this, "but he made up for it with some excellent cuddling." This comparison is a little jarring. Naturally her date couldn't match up to her living out a sexual fantasy, it's an unfair comparison. But I give a nod to encourage the conversation, still working though my baguette.

Riya's phone, which had been strategically placed on the table in her field of vision, starts to flash and she acknowledges a notification on the screen. "Right, that's my lunch over, I need to get back to the computer room before Sylvia loses her shit," she collects the remnants of her lunch and stands up. "Give me a text later if you want to pop over, I'm not doing anything apart from catching up on that Scandi drama you hate." I agree to give her a call when I am leaving for the day.

Riya hurries back to her office, and I sit for a few more minutes swirling the dregs of my coffee and downing the final gritty mouthful. I am about to head back myself when I hear a familiar tune and realise that *my* phone is ringing. I don't recognise the number flashing on the screen but answer out of curiosity.

"Please may I speak to Nicole Harris?" the voice enquires.

"This is Nicole, who's calling please?"

"This is Ellen from Ryan's Bookbinding," it takes me a second to make the connection to the Vie Lab, then my heart rate quickens. "I'm ringing to let you know that we have had a last-minute cancellation so could bring forward your appointment to 6pm tonight, if this works for you?" I barely notice the peculiar way she is talking; I only register the word *tonight.*

"Yes, of course," I reply a little too loudly, afraid that somehow my phone will lose connection and someone else will get the slot.

"Great. I'll email over the details now. Please do reply if you have any questions."

Ellen hangs up, and I gawk at my phone in disbelief. Tonight seems very close, and I get a sudden rush of apprehension. An email notification appears on the screen; I open it and scan the brief message. It is barely a message, just a few points to confirm what I already know. The address of the lab, the time of the appointment and the confidential nature of the project. Then at the very end, a disclaimer.

"Due to the last-minute nature of this cancellation, this scenario will be taken from another client's schema. The prewritten script has been deemed suitable for a general audience. We hope you will enjoy the experience."

My stomach churns as I re-read the email; experiencing someone else's scenario is unsettling. Though perhaps the scenario was particularly suitable for a newbie and that's why they rang me. My thoughts flick back and forth until I realise that I am over-analysing the situation; if I want to see the project first hand tonight, I have to accept the unknown.

4

As I leave the psych block at 4pm, I call Riya to tell her about tonight. I expect her to be disappointed that I am bailing on our plans, but she doesn't seem to care; probably pleased that I'll have some juicy details to divulge when we did meet up, rather than another one-way Q&A. Riya does however ask if I am OK as I sound "disturbingly out of breath". This is because I am practically jogging home, and am horrendously nervous, but I tell her that I've just got a bit of a cold and try to stifle my breathing as I round up the conversation.

I arrive at the old textile mill that houses my flat in about fifteen minutes, then clang up the steel steps to the fourth floor. The flat has absorbed the warmth of the day and feels stifling after the power walk. I crack open a few windows to air out the living room then head for the bathroom. Nerves started to coalesce about the unknown scenario planned for the evening. I feel like I am preparing for a mysterious blind date.

My hair is too thick and curly to wash and dry in an hour, so I don a plastic cap and shave my legs and armpits in the shower. Half way through, this notion strikes me as absurd. It doesn't matter if my legs are prickly; technically no-one is going to touch them. But somehow, I feel prepared with smooth legs. My pubic hair is on the verge of being bushy, but it seems presumptuous and a little ridiculous to shave it. There is also something protective about genital hair that I am reluctant to surrender.

The small bathroom quickly fills with hot, damp air. I wrap up in a large towel and dash across the corridor to my bedroom, escaping the humidity that will make my hair blow up. The handful of make-up items that I own are permanently strewn across the dresser in my room, I eye up each piece and wonder where to draw the line for this unknown scenario. Foundation is essential to prevent the inevitable blush from showing. Mascara and tinted lip balm may make me look less tired. Eyeliner might be overkill.

I try to pat down my curls with some mousse, but they spring back resolutely. I decide to revisit the hair situation once dressed. Pulling open the top drawer, I rifle around the cotton briefs for the nice silky ones I bought for a date about a year ago. Even though I know the scenario might not require visibility of my underwear, I want to be prepared for any eventuality. A flutter of heart palpitations commence as I consider how I'd feel about a sexual encounter in front of a stranger. There was always the *end game* option if things got too uncomfortable; the opportunity to experience immersive virtual reality seems worth potential awkwardness of escaping.

Hopefully.

I pick out a knee-length, mustard coloured dress that makes me look daring. Or so my mum had said last summer. Though perhaps she had meant the colour was daring. Either way, I need to project some courage. I apply lipstick, but quickly dab it off. No point giving myself something else to be conscious of. Having run through all the preparatory steps I can think of, I acknowledge my grumbling tummy and wonder whether to make a snack. My phone indicates that I have fifteen minutes until I should leave, and a barrage of social notifications. I dig out a cereal bar from the kitchen cupboard and sit by the window to flick through the pending conversations, firing back one-handed emojis and short sentence replies as holding messages. I will dedicate proper time to my friends after the appointment, when my mind is less jangled.

Though the lab is less than half an hour away, I set off a little early, so I don't have to get a sweat on. I bring my trench coat in case the Manchester rain catches me out. To take my mind off the nerves, I plug into my favourite podcast about mental health and consider the effects of nutritional supplementation on depression with a panel of experts.

Arriving at Ryan's Bookbinding and zoning out of the psych podcast at the same time is a bad idea Everything is too quiet and surreal. I almost wish that Riya was here for reassurance. Out of habit, I check my phone again, but nothing has changed since I left the flat. I take a long breath, press the buzzer next to the old shop door, and exhale too quickly as the nerves flood in. Ellen's voice snaps though the speaker:

"Sorry, Ryan's Bookbinding is closed."

I wonder how many non-clients have even pressed the buzzer.

"It's Nicole, I have that, erm, project," I suddenly realise my hands are empty, I haven't brought anything that looks like I am getting a book bound. "To pick up!" I add in quickly, but the door is already humming for me to enter. *What a rookie error!* I curse as I climb the stairs.

I enter the waiting room and Ellen is at the reception desk expecting me. She acknowledges my empty hands.

"I should have mentioned to bring a folder or something," Ellen says, and my face flushes up from the neck. "It doesn't really matter, just looks a bit odd if anyone sees you out of hours," she continues, registering my reddening face. "We're trying to fly under the radar until we set up a better space to work in."

Ellen turns her attention to the computer and recites the preparatory material.

"OK, so we're doing a 30-minute scenario. It's classed as a level one programme, a very standard request," Ellen glances across to read my face, evidently I looked nervous. "Do you want to know the details of the scenario?"

I want to seem unfazed in front of Ellen, but simmering anxiety makes me nod my head. Ellen smiles and says, "It's just a skydive replication," my limbs uncoil, "it's usually part of the induction scenario, but some clients really take to it and request it as a regular session." The flood of relief quickly curdles into a knot of regret. Deep down I had prepared myself for a sexual scenario, whether I was ready for it or not, and I couldn't help feeling a little let down by the change of plan. I try to neutralise this with a bright smile.

Ellen doesn't seem to notice as she pulls a clipboard from a shelf under the table. "If you could just fill out this health and safety form before we begin, please, that'd be great – feel free to take a seat over there," she indicates to the sofa.

I politely sit on the pristine sofa and look over the form. The first page is standard personal details: address, next of kin, medical history. Overleaf is an extensive confidentiality agreement. The last page is a little bit more unusual; entitled "General phobias and strong dislikes" with a sentence explaining that "all known strong reactions to stimuli should be stated in this section." I couldn't think of any off the top of my head. Studying psychology for so long had quashed a lot of my irrational fears, and an unease around wasps seemed too dull to list. Besides I could always end the game if there was an unexpected wasp-related story twist.

I tick and scrawl through the form as fast as I can, itching to get into the lab. "I think I'm finished," I say, springing back to the reception desk where Ellen is quietly typing. She pauses to skim through my responses. Tonight, her blonde bob is wavy; she absently flips a section of hair to the other side of her head as she reads.

"Great, we're all set," she says, her professional smile slipping back in. "You know the drill, let's go through to the control room." She leads the way to the adjoining room and taps the various computer terminals to life. I remember that the next part was to set down my affects, but I wait to be told every step just in case I mess something up. Ellen is typing a few notes into the left-most terminal.

"You can leave your things on this chair here," she says, patting the one next to her. "The programme will take a minute to load when you enter the room so just be prepared for the lights to change."

I nod and place my bag and coat on the chair. Then it occurs to me that I am not dressed for sky diving. "Do I need to get changed or anything?" I ask, wishing I'd worn trainers instead of pumps.

"Oh no you're fine in whatever," Ellen replies, tapping away without looking at me. "The system adapts so you'll have everything you need. You could go in naked, and it would account for that."

I try to unpick this, but my understanding starts to unravel when I think about the computer adjusting to my input. Then an alarming thought occurs to me,

"Wait, can I get hurt in the Vie Lab?" I ask, recalling the very real pleasure Riya seemed to experience.

Ellen makes a small noise, like a half-committed laugh, then finishes typing and turns around to face me. "Not unless you want to. The programme has very strict parameters around pain simulation, we have to override them to allow you to feel discomfort." She folds her arms and leans back into the chair a little, more casually that I had seen her sit before. "Don't worry, it's all completely safe. That's part of the charm." Her face displays a compromised smile, like she's disappointed I asked.

After a quiet moment where she seems to wait for further questions, and I offer none, she wheels back to her usual position and becomes engrossed in the set-up procedure. Even though the silence verges on impolite, I admire her fastidious concentration; it reminds me of all the hours I'd spent embroiled in my PhD write up, even down to the rigid loping of the shoulders typing away. When Ellen swings around to face me again I flinch realising that I have been staring at her. She smiles, dropping the pressed professionalism briefly, and points towards the door on the left. "Ready for you to enter now," she says, and her eyes crinkle. I wonder if she only truly enjoys this element of her job.

I oblige and depress the handle; the door is heavier than it looks. Inside, the whitewashed room seems much larger, and I notice that the one-way glass is well concealed. It feels more contained from the inside. Ellen's voice echoes in from the ceiling.

"Nicole, can you hear me?" I nod towards where I imagine Ellen is sat. "OK, great. Remember to exit the scenario, just say 'end game'. The lights will drop now, OK? Show me thumbs up or down?"

My nerves must be showing. I fake a wide smile whilst I hold up two thumbs up to the invisible window. The lights drop, and though I am expecting it, I feel vulnerable immersed in the transitory darkness. As the lights click back on, my body takes a second to adjust to the new and very different situation.

And then I feel unsteady, as though no longer stood on the solid ground of the white room. Trying to latch onto the current situation, I realise that I am sat in a small jump plane. My brain tries to track back to how I ended up wearing a bright red jumpsuit, I touch my face, and goggles. It's like I've launched straight into a dream, but with the lucid clarity of a real-life high-stress situation. The colours and sounds of the environment are overpowering. I look to my left, someone else wearing a red jumpsuit is also strapped tight into a passenger seat. They twist to face me.

"Nearly at optimal altitude," they shout over the rumbled of the plane. I can't see much of their face beneath the large goggles, but a thick beard covers their chin. I plan to reply but cannot form the words. Shock, or amazement, has stripped me right back to basic comprehension. Struggling for words, I nod, and they turn away. My brain cannot comprehend how the dimensions of the whole plane could fit in the small lab room. I must have passed out; this must be a dream. I bite my lip hard. It doesn't hurt, but I feel it.

Radio voices buzz in my ear out of nowhere, "Twelve thousand feet Pete, Nicole, we're ready to go," and then another voice, "Roger that, we're set to launch." The person next to me, presumably Pete, stands and points at my seat belt, "Time to unclip and head out," he barks, trying to drown out the overwhelming noise that is rushing in from a newly opened hatch. But I can't unclip myself, I am frozen to my seat, trepidation coursing through my veins. Skydiving has never been on my bucket list, but I didn't anticipate such a strong reluctance to try it out. The scenario seems to slow down around me, the whooshing air reducing to a light breeze and the sounds drifting further away. The radio earpiece is whispering inaudible instructions, but I can't grasp onto them. I wonder if I am waking up, though the sensation is more like passing out.

Then a jolt of awareness reminds me that I cannot get hurt. Whether I am dreaming, or in the Lab, the situation is all in my head anyway. I might as well embrace it. Everything rushes back at once and I unclip myself, raising unsteadily to my feet. I am supported towards the door by Pete. He stands next to me shouting for me to "Sit, one leg at a time," which only makes sense because he is miming what to do. I perch on the edge of the hatch, gripping the door frame. My stomach lurches at the scene that comes into view. We are in the misty expanse high above miles of patchwork fields. The wispy clouds blend into a distant glow so that everything appears endless.

I feel a tap on my shoulder and a yell of "Go now!" I don't let myself process my options, just push myself out of the plane. Immediately I begin to nosedive, then somersault back around catching sight of the plane lifting away, then flip back onto my front. After a few unsettling turns, I manage to right myself into the classic skydiving position I'd seen on TV.

"Doing great," a voice in my ear reassures me. I wonder whether they heard my stream of expletives as I rolled from the plane. Then realise that I don't know how any of the equipment works and panic. I try to ask how to launch my parachute, but the drop is literally taking my breath away with the wind. Even so, I get a reply.

"Don't deploy the parachute yet, you'd catch an air current and get swept away. Just enjoy the free fall. Pete will help you release when the time comes."

I try to relax and remember that this is all planned. I am just supposed to enjoy the sensations. Which are currently a mixture of rising bile, popping ears, and an overwhelming urge to squeal. I ride a thirty-second-long sensation like the plummeting path of a rollercoaster before beardy Pete appears by my side. He mimes moving his right hand to his backside and pulling. Over my headphones the disembodied voice tells me to "Keep my left arm raised and pull the toggle with my right." I fumble for the handle with my large-gloved hands and pull as instructed. I am immediately jerked back into an upright position. The scenery swings its perspective, and I can see the stretches of fields all around. The ground no longer rushes at me, then my heart rate slows down. I see Pete in the distance, his parachute deployed too, he gives me the thumbs up.

The air still streaks past my ears noisily, causing the skin on my face to ripple, but things feel more peaceful. Beneath my feet, the ground coasts reassuringly closer. The queasy swirl in my stomach subsides and the adrenaline levels off to a pleasant hum of elation. Now I can see why people might want to redo this scenario. It is incredible.

As the earth we are heading towards closes in, I am instructed by my ear piece to try and run on landing, "Like at the end of a zip wire." This has little applicability to me as I have never zip-wired, but I try to replicate the motion of running as my feet very quickly hit the hard ground. I trip up after a couple of wrong footings and roll into my parachute. It doesn't hurt at all. I laugh loudly at the silliness of it all, but no-one is around to join in. I bat free of the parachute material and stand up. But weirdly, the space is completely barren, and there is no sign of Pete or the plane. The air is deafeningly quiet now without the rushing wind. I wait to see if anything else happens, but it appears to be the conclusion of the story. Unsteadily, I shout, "End game," and then, abruptly, darkness closes the scene.

5

The lights flicker back on, and I hear Ellen's voice talking to me from a distance. I can barely catch the words; my brain is wading through soup. The door to the control room has reappeared and I lurch towards it, trying to gather my thoughts.

I am surprised to see that Ellen is sat facing the door when I enter. I was so used to seeing her profile or back tapping away at the computer that her face looks unfamiliar. Softer than the half-frowning image I had painted on my mind's eye, her expression milder.

"Did you like it?" she asks, her tone oddly keen. One of her hands is massaging the other. I try not to think of the repetitive strain injury she must endure from typing so quickly.

"It was incredible!" I reply, and her face lights up. "Definitely in a bit of a brain fog now though."

"Oh yeah that's normal. Takes a few goes to get used to the transition. It's a little bit like being shook awake, isn't it?"

I nod and dig my knuckles into the corners of my eyes. The adrenal fatigue is overcoming my excitement. I open my mouth to say "Yes," but the noise turns into a massive yawn. "God I am sorry that's really rude," my eyes water with the enthusiasm of the stretch.

Ellen laughs, a spry melodic laugh that doesn't quite suit her voice. "Don't worry, the first session ruins everyone – and they've normally had training to prepare."

I think of the free fall and how I hadn't been shown any of the protocols beforehand. "I've just realised how odd it is that I did a sky dive without any training. I feel quite pleased with myself." And I do; I've never done anything that precarious before.

"Ah yes, we normally do the sky dive as training," Ellen says, her face still pleasantly creased "There's a full hour session of running through the correct positioning and emergency procedures. It's all arbitrary though, nothing bad can happen to you. People just like to be psychologically prepared."

"Weren't you worried that I'd freak out? You know, free fall to my death or something?" I feel slightly perturbed by her casualness.

Again, the jingly laugh, and a little shudder of satisfaction runs across my chest. "Honestly, I was curious about how a person would react without preparation," she looks me straight in the eyes. "Though I nearly pulled the plug when you froze on the plane. I thought I'd made a big mistake!" She stands and leads me to the door as the lights drop down in the control room.

"You did really well though, it was interesting to watch." Ellen continues, walking around the reception desk and leaning on one elbow. "Perhaps next time we could try something different?"

I can't tell if she is being playful. Back in the bright lights of the reception room, the softness of her face seems to diffuse back to the medical neutrality.

"I'd love to! If you can fit me in again that'd be great."

Ellen seems to enjoy my enthusiasm, her face crinkling a little. "Well, I didn't actually cancel your appointment in three weeks, so we could stick with that?"

"Yes please," I nod, a shameless keen bean.

"Perfect," her face is cool, but a smile creeps in as I linger. "See you then."

6

As soon as I leave the building, I feel slightly sick; overexcitement combined with exhaustion. I can see now why Riya drove here. My pace on the way home is slow, my legs filled with sand like after a brutal spin class.

To keep my brain awake, I try to marry together my knowledge about neurostimulation and the Vie Lab experience, but none of the technology I know of fits the experience I just had. Even the transcranial magnetic stimulation machine at the University requires close proximity to the subject for even basic neuronal manipulation. My head swirls, and I wonder whether it's blood sugar crash. There are loads of takeaways on the way home, but I deviate slightly to go via my favourite pizza place Stefano's; they bake the absolute best veggie supreme. My stomach growls as I stand by the window waiting for service, and order three rather than my normal two slices. The guy who serves me looks new, and I'm glad I don't have to make small talk as I am keen to shove the pizza in my face and get to bed.

By the time I get home I feel rejuvenated. I have a stream of messages on my phone from Riya, but I need to wash and change before I can relax. The free fall situation left me sticky, and I'm sure I've rubbed mascara all around my eyes. I abandon my coat and bag by the front door and jump in the shower for the second time this evening. This time, I make the effort to wash and condition my mane. It is so nice to stand under the hot stream and relax; my muscles slowly unclenching.

I wrap up in a dressing down, even though it is a little too hot for summer, and shuffle into the living room. I remember there are some ice cream cones in the freezer and retrieve one for a phone snack. I flop across the sofa, ear buds wedged in, and call Riya. She answers after five agonising rings.

"So how was it?" Riya opens, then the phone connection crackles.

"Where are you? I can barely hear you." I raise my voice over the static.

"I'm just at home, hang on," there is a series of ruffled noises then silence. "How about now?" the line is clear again.

"That's better, what did you do?" I ask, rolling onto my side to eat the ice cream more easily.

"Just moved onto the balcony, the flat gets bad reception sometimes," I picture her stood next to her potted herbs on the small urban garden she'd created outside her living room. "Please divulge," she encourages.

"Oh my god, where to start!" I try to rein in my excitement, but it is hard, I just want to rattle everything off in one long sentence. "It's amazing isn't it - I can't believe that none of it is real!"

"Well, I don't know about real," Riya laughs, "perception is reality after all!"

This trips me up. Theoretically she is right; many of the things we are taught in psychology often boil down to this. A reductionist approach of course, but it holds weight here.

"So, your mystery experience?" she urges after a pause.

I start to recount the free fall experience, but she interrupts as soon as she recognises the scenario. "Oh yes, I did that one as my training session – Pete and Ethan showing you the ropes of skydiving. Bit of a snore. Still, I nearly pissed myself when I jumped out of the plane," Riya shrieks and I tip my head to one side automatically, though I can't flinch away from the earbuds.

"Glad it wasn't just me," I lie, deciding on the spot that I shouldn't mention skipping the actual training. It just feels a bit off.

"I haven't got another session for ten days though, that's ageees." She sighs, and the feeling resonates.

"Urgh, I know, I'm not in for three weeks. You could definitely get addicted to the sessions, couldn't you?" I say, then take a bite from the cone.

"Yeah, like adrenaline junkies," Riya agrees. "But with the added power of being able to describe exactly how you want the scenario to go." She pauses then says, "Hey I wonder if that's why they space out the appointments."

"I thought the gap was because of the development time?" I frown even though Riya can't see my face. Ice cream is dripping onto the sofa.

"Well, you don't actually have to submit your idea until like a week before your appointment."

I wondered whether Riya had already planned her next scenario. I press her on this.

"Of course! I've had the idea for ages. You can come and see it in the flesh if you like? Though I guess, not in the literal sense!" she laughs at herself again.

I hesitate for a second. It doesn't seem healthy to repeatedly delve into the depths of a friend's fantasies. But something inside me yearns for another visit to the lab, and the chance to ask Ellen more questions.

"Wouldn't Ellen mind if I keep tagging along?" I ask.

"Nah, she didn't care last time did she," I almost contradict her, then realise that might make her retract the offer. "Just don't touch any of her fancy dials! The session is on Friday eleventh of August, put it in your diary now. I know what you're like for forgetting dates." She yawns. "Oh man, I should head back inside it's getting chilly. Catch you tomorrow?"

As she hangs up, I glance up at the calendar on the wall and realise I haven't changed the month over from July yet. I stand up and flip the page to August, then see I have a reminder for this Friday: "Ballet with Connor." I wince; Riya is right about me forgetting dates. Anything beyond the next couple of days seemed inscrutable to me. I just don't map time very well.

My friend from undergrad, Connor, had booked tickets for us to go to the ballet months ago. At the time it seemed like a great idea, but then it totally slipped my mind. I message him quickly to check he was still up for it. His almost immediate reply made it clear that he was indeed up for it, and very much looking forward to it. He then proceeded to check that I had remembered the date. My reputation precedes me.

The idea of ballet now seems boring, but realistically I need something to take my mind of this new obsession; I couldn't just fester over the Vie Lab for three solid weeks. Especially without running it through a search engine.

Just as I plan to switch my phone to night mode, an email from the Vie Lab lights up the screen. I hurriedly flick it open in full. The address says Ryan's bookbinding but even that name gave me the same thrill as the lab now. The message was a carbon copy template providing detailed instructions for scenario submission. I read it eagerly, keen to build out the plan in my head.

I needed to submit my scenario to them at least one week before my appointment to give them time to develop it. The submission could either be a two-page (maximum) description of the session I wanted, or I could just give general ideas with some room for improvisation by the developer. The scenario could be anything I wanted it to be, but if I chose to work with restricted topics on an attached list I would need to sign a disclaimer to take responsibility for the nature of the code. There was also a strictly prohibited, off-limits list. This made me shudder a little. How far did people want to push it? Curiously, I click to open the list of restricted topics.

Clients will be made to sign a legal waiver form if they wish to address topics including, but not limited to, the following:

BDSM (bondage, dominance, sadism, masochism) sex

Penetration from non-standard sex toys

Erotic asphyxiation and or strangulation

Violence

Clients are prohibited from submitting scenario requests on the following themes:

Child cruelty or pornography

Animal cruelty or pornography

Necrophilia

Cannibalism

Incest

Murder

I close the document with a sick feeling in my stomach. I wonder whether the list had been generated from client requests they'd had to reject, or whether it had been written to prevent weird applications in the first place. Hopefully the latter. I guess if you are allowing people to explore their wildest fantasies, you must make sure you're not opening yourself up for any moral or legal disputes.

I did note that most of the banned topics were sexual, which made me wonder if a large number of the requests were sex related. My own sexual desires feel very ordinary and unimaginative, nothing I'd have to live out in virtual reality in any case. It had never really occurred to me to wonder what else might turn me on outside of the regular sexual preamble I'd experienced. Though the frequency of my sex encounters could no longer be classed as *regular*.

I grab a notebook from the coffee table and flip to a fresh page, flopping back down to the sofa to deliberate. I write the word "Ideas" and underline it. Then pause, tapping the pen top against my teeth for a few moments before writing "1.

Women?" This is true at least; I had thought of women in a sexual way. Though I tried to push the unsettling image of Riya sitting in the 'doctor's office' out of my mind. And then my mind jumps to Ellen; of her reading my request, knowing my desires, creating an intimate scenario for me. A tingling heat creeps up my neck in anticipation.

7

The next few days blur together as I get sucked into academia. Participant data comes in unexpectedly from trials and it is a real mess. After half a day of tidying the spreadsheets and unpicking brain stats, the analysis starts to get interesting, and I find myself rooted to the desk. It is exhilarating to feel drawn into the work again. But by Friday I am exhausted, with a lower back niggle from sitting down so much. I'm desperately looking forward to a weekend of switching off. I almost forget my date with Connor as I fast track my plans to running a bath and pouring a crisp gin and tonic. Thank god for calendar alerts.

I text Connor confirming plans to meet at the theatre and take a detour on the walk home to pick up chow mein. Queuing in the Chinese takeaway, I suddenly realise how hungry I am after working through lunch. The woman at the counter reads my mind and hands me my order with the noodle box open, chopsticks poking out of the top ready to eat. I snaffle the food on the walk home, enjoying every salty mouthful at top speed. As I try desperately to pinch up the tiny morsels at the bottom of the box, all of the food seems to hit my stomach at once. A heavy, stuffed feeling descends; not ideal for the one night I plan to get dressed up.

Back at my flat I make a cup of peppermint tea and sit on the couch to sip it slowly, hoping to ease the bloated feeling before I choose an outfit. I scroll through my phone apps absent-mindedly, absorbing the stream of Friday-night activities that people I know, or do not know, have got planned. There is a buzz of enthusiasm as the nine-to-fivers shed their work persona and gear up for two days of unrestrained endeavours. The hype is contagious, and I start to feel more excited about having plans myself. I consider declaring the ballet trip to my social network but quickly decide against it. If I ever post anything to the internet, I usually become obsessed with intermittently checking the reaction it gets.

After a ten-minute rest, I prise myself off the sofa to browse my clothes. My wardrobe is a repetitive rail of white shirts and black jeans with a smattering of dresses. When I got the lectureship job at the University, I panicked myself about what I would wear every day to look smart but not overdone. I found a great shirt and jean combination and decided that this would do as an everyday uniform, so bulk bought ten white shirts and four pairs of black jeans. For the past year, I haven't pondered an outfit choice for work, and laundry has been a breeze, but now picking what to wear for events becomes an unreasonably stressful decision.

After flicking the hangers of clothes back and forth several times, the best I can pull together is a structured, navy-blue dress I bought for a conference dinner two years ago and flat, silver pumps. A little red lipstick perks up my tired looking face. I add an extra couple of layers of mascara to my eyes to widen them. There isn't much I can do with my hair, so I just smooth a few strands down with water. I step back to review the ensemble in the full-length mirror by the bed, not bad for a quick turnaround. And still enough time to walk into town.

◆◆◆

Connor is waiting for me outside the theatre, looking sharp in a dark grey suit. As I approach, I mentally turn over a couple of outdated jokes about gay men having good taste, but I know he won't appreciate any of them. He'd probably tell me his sexual preference had nothing to do with his innate sense of style. Instead, I kiss his smooth-shaven cheek, tell him he looks dapper, then let him lead me up the stairs through the crowds of finely dressed folk.

Ballet and theatre are two things I enjoy attending, when I am there, but would have lost touch with a long time ago without Connor. We met in university, at the Art Society. I'd only intended to go along to enquire about pottery classes but found myself drawn into the peaceful energy of the studios. There people worked quietly, absorbed in their creative worlds, drawing inspiration from one another and the paint splattered art books splayed around the room. I looked forward to Thursday evenings in the basement studios; two solid hours of people congregating to work on their projects and whisper about ideas they'd had.

Connor drew my attention when he showed up halfway through second term, all angular features and graceful poise.

He brought his own sketchbook, an armful of heavy art books, set himself up in the corner as though he'd always been there, and busied himself recreating the scenes laid out in front of him. After observing him from afar for about a month, I decided to put myself in his circle of influence. One week I arrived early to the session and sat in his regular seat, trying to be cool about it, but as soon as he arrived my whole face flamed, and I laughed loudly, a horrible nervous habit that sometimes flared up. Everyone turned to see what was so funny. Connor was bemused by my sudden outburst and sat next to me, laughing with me as though at a private joke. I was in love with him, and would be for months, even after discovering he only had eyes for men.

To this day Connor remains one of my most culturally involved friends. He was refreshing to speak to in contrast to my work friends who seemed consumed by their research. Connor worked in accounting, but barely ever talked about work. He insisted that accounting was utterly dull and that he never let it cross his mind without payment. His spare time was filled with an increasing variety of creative hobbies, regularly attending sessions for pottery, painting and creative writing. He also kept a passion for performing arts alive by making sure he always had tickets for shows that passed through Manchester. I was pleased that he kept asking me along.

"Nicole, you are looking very lovely tonight," Connor tells me he as we wait in line at the theatre entrance, he looks at me straight on. "That red lipstick really suits your skin tone." I feel my face flush to match; compliments about makeup always make me feel self-conscious. I resist the urge to touch my face.

"Shall we get some wine before the performance starts?" I ask as soon as we enter the grand lobby of the theatre, the gold painted furniture and plush red fabrics, making me aware of my sloppy posture among the refined gathering. I need to relax into it more.

"Or champagne perhaps, to get in the mood?" He replies, arching his right eyebrow provocatively. I feel a tingle of reminiscence of how besotted I once was with his charm.

"Definitely champagne," I say, "but I'll leave the wine choice up to you."

"Too right," he replies, "You can't spend your whole life drinking the second cheapest bottle of wine."

"Come on, everyone knows that's the best choice." I smile, whilst he shakes his head, trying not to look amused.

I prop myself at the bar whilst he orders, glancing around at the room filling with people in their formal attire. I realise I am underdressed for the occasion, but I don't envy the women swooping around in their long, fussy dresses. My dress is more comfortable than they look.

"Here we go," Connor says, passing over a tall glass of champagne, then tipping his own to clink them together "cheers to us, and eight years of friendship!"

I freeze "My god is it really eight years?" I peer at the glass whilst I mentally calculated the time that has passed and realise he is right.

"Time flies, eh?" Connor gracefully sips his champagne, looks over my shoulder to survey the room then returns his gaze to me, all in one seamless movement. I know this habit well; for some reason, he fills gaps in conversations with a quick assessment of the room. After completing the check, he returns his attention to you, undivided, to start the next topic. I used to think he was assessing the single men in the room, but now he has a long-term boyfriend I just assume it is an old habit.

I ask how his painting is going, whether he has finished the portrait of his friend he'd been working on when we met up a few months ago. He has in fact just finished the portrait and is looking for a new project.

"I like the idea of getting back into life drawing again. I'd like to try a nude in oils," he continues "I'm inspired after going to the Virginia Howl exhibition in London last month. I think you would have enjoyed the show, it reminded me a little of the portraits you used to paint." My painting days feel like a million years ago, I haven't even touched a brush since I started my PhD. Connor muses for a moment then says, "I'll lend you the book I bought about the exhibition, it's very good."

I remember reading about Virginia Howl and her work, but I don't keep up with what's happening in the art world these days. It makes me feel quite sad to realise that I'm not making time to visit exhibitions any more. Years ago, I was always looking for galleries and shows to explore; but then at some point it just stopped occurring to me to go.

"Yeah, I'd be interested to have a read," I say. Connor looks mildly surprised by my enthusiasm.

"Great, I'll drop it at your flat on my way home from work next week then." He says, eyebrow slightly cocked as he sips his champagne again.

People start to gather around the exit of the bar indicating that the performance is about to commence. We finish our glasses and join the queue, shuffling into the semi-dark theatre. Anticipation for the show fires up an excited tingle in my middle. We find our seats and sit down. I turn to glance at Connor in the darkness, his strong features in silhouette. I have an urge to tell him about the Vie Lab and prove that I am still doing interesting things. I'm keen to know what he thinks of it all, what scenario he would choose, but the lights drop, and a hush descends on the audience.

In the moment of silence before the music starts, I realise that it would have been unwise to discuss the Vie Lab with Connor. As much as he might appreciate the concept, and would probably have some interesting thoughts on it, I need to respect that it is a confidential project.

I try to focus my attention on the stage.

The curtains lift, and a slender figure dressed in white sweeps onto the stage. We are close enough in the stalls that I can make out the lean muscles beneath her white tights. A skin-tight leotard covers her torso. She moves her limbs with such controlled fluidity that my eyes become transfixed, the rest of the stage a void. Presently, another dancer joins her onstage, a man wearing even fewer items of clothing. They move together seamlessly, lifting and propelling one another as though weightless. As they entwine and pull apart, I am enthralled by the dance. I had never truly thought about how sensual ballet is; the contours of the body, supple and fluid as the limbs come together, the intensity of every movement.

I glance sideways to Connor, but he is fully absorbed in the performance. I try to reengage myself in the same way, but my mind is now elsewhere, planning.

8

Connor cajoles me into a few drinks at The Duke Bar after the show. I loosen up with the alcohol and jovial atmosphere, and soon find myself guiding conversations toward the realms of the Vie Lab, desperately wanting to share the secret with someone. I shift the topic before I let any details slip and instead introduce Ellen as if she is someone new at work; I call her Melanie. Still getting a sense of satisfaction talking about the project in an indirect way, describing Ellen and her interest in neuropsychology, the habit she has of scooping hair out of her face, every detail I can recall that doesn't require the lab. Connor sits with pressed lips and raised eyebrows.

"Sounds like you've got a workplace crush," he shouts over the music, leaning in closer to my ear, "good luck with that!" He flicks me a double thumbs-up, and then grimaces in dramatic sympathy. My face must be a picture, too sodden with alcohol to think up a quick-witted reply. But then not feeling a strong enough defence, bemused by his assumption. I smile coyly, allowing it to be interesting for him.

I ask him about his partner Rick and receive a long-winded story about their house-buying plans. I nod politely, pretending to care about the fluctuating interest rates and ISA options, secretly contemplating how ludicrous it is that we're trying to have this conversation over the thumping music of the bar. After what feels like a polite length of time, I wait for a break in conversation then pull at Connor's arm, ushering him onto the small square of dance space next to the bar. The space is already full of men, and a handful of women, throwing their limbs and gyrating their torsos to the house music. I don't know the songs, but the rhythm is predictable enough and soon Connor and I are as sweaty as everyone else; laughing absurdly at our formal outfits in the sea of tight jeans and fitted t-shirts.

Connor is hilarious to dance with, so much energy and zest. His normally tight posture switches to freely comical as he throws himself into the music. I flash back to the excited energy of our nights out together in university; the times he dragged me to gay nights in the city when everyone else had gone home for holidays, but we stayed one extra weekend for the freedom. All the nights out merging together into one hazy night of jumping, sweating and laughing. I need to make more time for this.

When I get home, many hours later and with a good few glasses of champagne in my system, I feel it might be a very good idea to write down my new Vie Lab idea. I snatch up the notebook from the living room and huddle it into the bedroom with me, giggling at how big my hair looks as I pass the living room window. I strip off my dress and bra, and flop into bed. My eyes are so heavy with the anticipation of sleep, but I manage to scrawl my ideas from the ballet into the book before sliding into a gently spinning slumber.

9

The next day I wake up late and sore. As I shuffle onto my elbows, I notice the red lipstick smudges on my pillow and remember my hasty notes on the bedside table. I cringe reading back what I wrote before I drifted off:

Sexy ballet. Clothes peel off. Man and woman, the dance from the opening act.

Somehow this lacks the imaginative detail I felt that I had fabricated. I sit in bed for a while, quiet and crossed legged, rewriting and rethinking the idea. After about an hour, I feel that I am getting close to something decent; an idea I actually feel excited about. I pick up my phone, cast a quick look over the notifications, then start to craft an email message to Ellen. I want to send my scenario before I overthink it and crush my idea with self-consciousness. There is something profoundly embarrassing about explaining a fantasy. I try to think of all of the other people who have done just this, decided that want to experience something they may never have chance to in their real life. I feel a pang of jealousy at all of those who have come before me, managing to share their desires without shame and reap the benefit of experience. How they have all shared something with Ellen, and she has created something unique for them. I type quickly, and press send without re-reading. My insides squeeze with excitement and trepidation, then gurgle with hunger.

◆ ◆ ◆

Two hours later, as I am collecting shirts and towels for the wash, I flip over my phone out of habit. There is a reply from Ellen. I drop my bundle of laundry and hastily flick open the message.

"Hi Nicole. Thanks for sending this over, it sounds like an interesting idea. Would you like to meet and discuss in person, flesh out the scenario together? I'm free tonight. Ellen."

Not the reply I was expecting, but intriguing. The tone is professional, but an invitation to her house in the evening seems overly personal. I text Riya for some perspective:

"Hey! So, when you submitted your scenario did you give details or just an idea? And did you get invited to Ellen's place to discuss? x"

No point beating around the bush. She replies quickly:

"VERY detailed. I know what I like ;) and NO I did not get an invitation for a session at Ellen's – did you?? Favouritism!"

A smug warmth rises in my chest knowing that I got invited to Ellen's and Riya didn't. I text her back to joke about being teacher's pet, then contemplate how to reply to Ellen.

I want to get as much time as possible on the project, and being the curious human I am, want to have a nosey at her house. But she is essentially a stranger, and there is something unsettling about going to a stranger's house. Though, I remind myself, Riya has no problem taking guys she met online back to her place, so perhaps I am being overly cautious.

I email Ellen back, a brief confirmation that I am free and a request for her address. I send the message, then scroll to reread her previous mail, a creeping excitement at the plan. Just as I am about to discard my phone, a text message appears from a new number.

"Hi, it's Ellen, my address is 37 Milling St. Feel free to call if you get lost. See you at 8?"

I get a rush of adrenaline reading the message and resist to urge to reply saying 'it's a date'.

For what feels like eternity, I busy myself with errands. I wash clothes, clean the flat, and plan a grocery list for the week. Remembering the comment from Riya about missing appointments, I transfer events from my phone dairy to my physical calendar on the wall where they seem more tangible. I am surprised by how quiet my next few weeks are looking, normally weekends get filled with meetups, weddings, family events and conferences months in advance. August feels vacuous; the freedom is intoxicating.

I shower early so I can let my hair dry naturally into springy curls, then return to my jeans and t-shirt to do some reading. Increasingly I was finding my Saturday evenings entailed reading research articles for work, drinking wine, then having a bath, sometimes a combination of the above. But today I was excited to dig into the manilla envelope that had sat on my desk at work, like an unopened present for the tail end of the week. I'd used my university library account to order several of Professor McAllister's research papers to swot up before my next session. Of course, I had mixed in some papers more directly related to my own research to side step any potential questions from the librarian.

In preparation for an hour or so reading, I brew a black coffee in a tiny moka pot and take it to the table by the window, laying down the thick envelope. Even though I know it's just a pile of printed research papers, something I see day in and out at work, I feel a greedy excitement opening the package. I slide the neat, white sheets out onto the table and flick my nails through the corners. There's a good few hours' worth of reading. Picking up the first batch of stapled sheets, I notice a yellow sticky note affixed to the top left corner. In neat, black handwriting it says, "Don't look too hard."

I re-read the note several times, confused, then thumb past the first page of the paper and see that the subsequent pages are blank. The next publication is the same, first page, intact but the rest is plain, white paper. I flick the entire stack together and see the same pattern throughout. Paranoia escalates into panic. Someone doesn't want me to read these papers. I consider ringing the library to find out who sent the package but realise that any questions that come up might breach confidentiality to the Vie Lab. Out of habit, I pick up my phone and debate a solution to my rising stress. I dial Riya's number and sit through several lengths of ringing before realising that it's Saturday and she is likely to be busy. I drop her a text instead.

"Hey, sorry for spamming you with calls. Just had something odd to discuss but we can catch up later! x"

Sending the text takes the edge off, and after a few minutes looking out of the window, sipping my coffee, I have rationalised the situation. If testers from the Vie Lab are picked from academia, then it is possible that someone from the University's library is involved. Perhaps they are just stopping me from breaching the contract that we signed. After a few embellishments on this story, I am convinced. I take the envelope of papers to the recycling pile and slide it beneath a cereal box.

I guess that Ellen is going to be my only way to learn more about the Lab.

10

A quick search on my map app shows that the walk to Ellen's is 30 minutes. I check the street image to make sure she doesn't live above a boarded-up shop too. Reassuringly, the photo shows a typical Manchester Victorian terrace house. I consider cycling over, but I can never relax with my bike chained outside someone's house. Besides I have plenty of time, and the evening looks warm and bright. I leave my flat and head out of town, walking against the currents of people streaming into the city for the night. Many of them loud and intoxicated already. The air is heavy with residual heat from the day and a warm glow of excitement starts to uncurl. I plug into the music on my phone and pick up the pace to Joy Division's *Unknown Pleasures*.

Ellen lives in the small residential collective just outside of town; rows upon rows of nearly identical redbrick terraces stand back-to-back. I turn down the road parallel to Ellen's initially, then backtrack with a feeling of déjà vu, and arrive at her gate just after eight. Perspiration prickles under my arms, and my face is flushed. I give myself a minute to relax and check my phone before knocking. No notifications, nothing to distract my racing thoughts with. I glance instead around the forecourt, notice how there are no pots or plants and wonder whether this means that Ellen is renting the place. This is something of a mental tic I developed after buying my flat; curious to know who else has bought and where. Always weighing up my commitment to a one bedroom in the city when many of my friends had moved to larger suburban houses.

The heavy front door starts to open then closes again. Scuffling starts behind the door and Ellen shouts, "Sorry, just a second," then opens the door halfway, looking unusually flustered. A large black dog head squeezes between her thigh and the door, letting out a bellowing *bouf*.

"Shush Ted!" she says, pushing the head back inside the house with her leg. "Sorry Nicole, he just likes to see who's at the door but he's completely harmless."

This is obvious as I step into the hallway and Ted immediately nudges his head beneath my hand so I will stroke him. I laugh and Ellen smiles, "Oh good, you like dogs!" The genuine grin on her face sends an unexpected ripple of delight through my stomach. "Come through to the living room," she urges "He'll stop harassing you when you're settled.

I kick off my trainers in the hall and follow Ellen down the hall to a room on the right. It looks like a living room, but the lack of a TV is disorientating. There are two large sofas up against plain, cream walls and a low coffee table in the middle of the room covered in paper and electronics. Beyond this a large dog bed in the corner and a vinyl player placed awkwardly on the floor.

I perch on the edge of the sofa closest to the door and Ted, a greying black Labrador, huffs down next to my feet so I can pet him again. Ellen sits down on the other sofa, then immediately stands up again.

"Would you like a drink?" She says, moving towards the door. "I've got tea, coffee or a bottle of wine in the fridge - I usually find this sort of work comes more naturally after a glass or two," there is a twinkle in her eye.

"Wine it is!" I say, trying to relax into a normal sitting position on the sofa. The deep back of the chair makes it difficult to sit upright properly. I slouch, then reconsider and perch again. Ellen promptly returns with a bottle of white wine and her laptop.

"Sorry forgot to ask what wine you drink? I'm having white, but I've also got a few different reds if that's what you'd prefer?"

"White is perfect thanks," I say, secretly pleased that she has picked white. Red wine tends to exacerbate my rosy cheeks.

"Fab, I'll grab some glasses!" Ellen places the bottle and laptop on the small coffee table. She seems like a totally different person outside of work; enthusiastic and energetic. I wonder how much her passive professionalism is part of the job. It probably puts people at ease to be within that air of medical neutrality.

Ellen comes back from the kitchen with glasses, bends over the coffee table shuffling around paper to make room for them, then pours a considerable amount of wine into each flute. She passes one to me, collects her own and sits down on the other side of sofa in front of the laptop. Then in quick succession she takes a large sip of wine, presses the power button on the laptop and shuffles it and herself closer to me. I get a rush of tingling nerves and become suddenly aware of my limbs, trying to hold myself so I don't accidentally touch Ellen. I take a large gulp of wine to ease the self-consciousness. Ellen busies herself opening files and terminals on the computer. I stoke Ted mechanically, until he grows tired of my relentless petting and takes himself to bed. I don't know what to do with my hands now, so find myself drinking again. When Ellen seems satisfied that sufficient windows are open, she picks up her glass and leans back to consider me.

"I thought your idea was interesting, very sensual," she says sipping her wine "but I wasn't sure whether you intended for the story to progress sexually? Do you want to interact with the characters, or did you just want to view a sexy ballet show?"

A warm blush tickles the edges of my face, coming up from my neck; I have not consumed enough wine for this question. Ellen doesn't appear to notice, as she ploughs on:

"So, I started coding the scenario based on your request, but that only takes up a quarter of the allocated time. Usually, I would go ahead and add in embellishments to flesh out the story, but I wasn't entirely sure if you wanted to get *involved*?" A tiny smile hangs on her lips, as though she enjoys the uncertainty, or the fun of pressing me for details.

I try to think how best to word my response; I want to see what Ellen would come up with for the scenario, and I do want it to be sexual, but I don't want to be so blatant about it. I drink more wine to fill the silence whilst I practice the sentence in my head.

"Getting involved would be interesting," I cringe at echoing her earlier words. "Though I quite like the idea of a surprise. Not knowing what is going to happen feels more realistic, if you know what I mean?"

Ellen's face lights up. "Oh, cool OK. I usually have to rein in my imagination writing the scenarios, most people are quite prescriptive. Don't want to mess up their chance to live out their fantasies." Ellen finishes her wine, then looks me straight in the eyes to say, "I got the feeling you'd be open to some improvisation."

The intensity of her eyes locking onto mine makes my pulse spike. The wine and adrenaline combination makes me confusingly relaxed and excited at the same time. A sensation that verges on arousal.

"Well if I'm going create a session with a surprise, I can't really expect you to help me write it," she snaps the lid of the laptop shut, but doesn't move away from me. Unsure where this was going, but worrying that she might suggest I leave, I decide to intervene.

"You could tell me about the background of the project?" I say, my voice cracking awkwardly.

Ellen seems to like this question and tops up both of our wines. The bottle is now empty. She leans back into the chair and crosses her legs. I notice a small hole in the kneecap of her leggings, the white skin poking through as she tucks her feet beneath her. I too lean back into the chair, pulling one leg up for balance against the recline.

"So, the programme itself was created by Professor Eric McAllister about 15 years ago. It was originally a side project to his theoretical research on virtual reality software. He is a computer scientist, we both are, but he is very prominent figure in the field." Ellen pauses to see if I am interested in this level of detail. "The Professor was testing out some hypotheses he had about brain-computer interfaces. I was working as a postgrad student on some of the projects at the time, we had similar interests, so I often got involved with his stuff." She stops to take a mouthful of wine; I catch a look in her eye that I can't quite place. Sadness? Disappointment? She continues:

Then about ten years ago, when he was looking into repurposing some other tech he'd been working on, figuring out how to code the scenarios in greater detail, he told me about the Vie Lab. Of course, I was immediately interested, and he offered me a job working for him, outside of the University. I had only just graduated at the time, so it was a good opportunity for me." Ellen looks over to Ted snoring in the corner, sips again then continues.

"By then he knew he had developed something interesting and important but was worried about how the technology might be abused, so he refrained from publishing any data from the project. We kept it as an exciting secret, working all hours to test its capabilities. I had written some complex code in my time, but we were pushing boundaries with the sensory involvement elements." She suddenly stops "Am I rambling?"

"Not at all, it's very interesting," I say, genuinely enthralled. Ellen looks pleased, seemingly enjoying being the centre of attention.

"Professor McAllister recently retired from the University, so we don't have the same connections to the facilities, but we don't really need it anymore, we're well beyond the theoretical and development phases. We have something tangible and testable. The intention was for Eric to have more free time to dedicate to the testing with me, but he seems to be enjoying travelling around to conferences instead, so I work alone a lot these days."

The last sentence twists out of her mouth almost reluctantly, so I jump in with a question to keep her momentum going.

"How long have you been testing the lab for?"

"Just over a year," Ellen says "We brought in a few trusted connections to be guinea pigs, and when we smoothed out the flaws, we opened it up to a wider audience. Eric is incredibly protective about the project, so the testers are rigorously checked out before they are brought on board."

I am about to ask what this entails but she streams on. "Apart from you. Though I guess you came highly recommended by Riya."

I feel a mixture of pride and jealousy. Still unable to shake that Riya was invited to the project when I wasn't. "How do you decide who to invite to the lab?" I ask, before I consider whether this would make me feel worse.

"Well, we had an idea of the sorts of people to invite. Eric was adamant that we stay within the academic circle as he places a lot of weight on their respect for confidentiality. We were sure to include some Psychologists because of the potential therapeutic directions the Vie Lab could take." My arm hairs flare up, this touches sensitivities about not being considered. But then nearly jump out my skin as Ted suddenly lets out a huge woof from the other side of the room.

"Oh sorry," Ellen says, looking at her watch. "Sometimes he does that if he needs to go out. He's quite old and set in his ways," she laughs and sets down her empty wine glass on the table. I do the same, disappointed by the abrupt end to the chat.

"Shall we walk you back to your place?" Ellen says, standing and smoothing her dress over her hips.

I thank her, looking forward to extending the conversation for the walk, but lamenting the end of wine. It was just at the point that I'd drank enough to fancy some more.

Sadly, as soon as we get outside, Ellen changes the topic from the Vie Lab to some dog-related tales from when Ted was a puppy. I laugh along, though keenly aware that the time for interesting conversation had passed. The walk is sobering, and by the time we reach my flat, Ellen and I are back to polite chat.

"This is me," I say, indicating to the large, red brick building. I pause for a second, deciding whether to invite her up, but Ellen cuts in:

"I miss living in the city," she cranes her neck back to take in the stacks of flats, then back down to me. "Thanks for coming over tonight, I feel very inspired to write your script." We are standing unnaturally close, but no particular action feels like the right way to end the night. So, I smile and say:

"Well text me if you need any more ideas."

She nods, smiling back as she leads Ted down the road. I let myself into the building, trying to stem a flood of analytical thoughts. The night has an ache of unanswered questions.

11

On Sunday I rise with a weird, cold feeling. The emptiness of the day stretches ahead of me, and I puzzle to think how to fill it. Weekends are an odd time for my friends. None of us live within walking distance from one another, so impromptu plans never happen; we schedule each other in. I have the day entirely to myself and my thoughts.

My flat is immaculate after yesterday's clean spree, so I grab my grocery list to check off my only remaining task. It is oddly reassuring to know that the local 24-hour supermarket will be open, and I can get my shopping done without having to wait for the superstore out of town to open. I prefer to avoid the crowds when possible.

The supermarket is predictably empty, 8am on a Sunday is an unsociable time to shop. I grab my essentials for the week, and some croissants for breakfast, then head back. The two streets I have to cross to reach my flat are quiet. Normally thronged with crowds of shoppers or drinkers, weekend mornings don't feel like Manchester. I see only a handful of people heading to work, all of them absorbed in their phones or breakfasts.

Back at the flat, I turn on the oven to warm a croissant, and bang yesterday's coffee grounds into the bin to make a fresh pot. I turn on my laptop and my mind wanders back to last night; debating whether Ellen will text about my scenario, or whether I will have to wait for the session to see what she has created. A small part of me wants to text her, to see if she wants to hang out again today, to continue yesterday's conversation. But I refrain and take the pot off the stove.

I sit at the table by the window with my breakfast and laptop, browsing recently uploaded videos from creators I subscribe to. I click on an upload from a Canadian artist who paints landscapes *en plein air*. It is relaxing to watch, and I normally tune in to unwind after work. Today, however, I pay more attention to the paints used, and techniques covered, recalling the canvasses I used to dedicate my spare time to. It's hard to remember how I lost the drive to paint. It must have happened in the transition from Undergraduate to PhD. As soon as my free time became my work time, I lost the dedication to hobbies. Eventually the confidence trickles away, and you consider the set-up time every time you have the inclination to paint. I glance around my small flat, wondering if I would have space to set up an easel. There is a small area at the end of the room, the corner between the window and the wall and I picture myself standing there, brush in hand, painting.

Once the idea is rooted, I grow more enthused. Closing my laptop and returning my plate to the kitchen area, I head to the bedroom to dig around in my chest of drawers. There is an array of sketchbooks; some large hardbacks, some pocket sized and flimsy. I withdraw an A4 black book and a tin of pencils then rock back onto my heels to flick through my old sketches. Nostalgia swims in as I turn the pages and see my old attempts at still life and landscapes. Further into the book I reach a collection of nudes from when I went to weekly life drawing classes. Some of the drawings are loose and quick, others intricate and fleshed out. None of them quite looking right on the page, I never did develop an eye for perspective.

I look to see what else remains in the drawer. There are a few medium stretched canvases and some flat looking tubes of paint. I twist the cap off blue azure acrylic and flakes scatter across my knees. The paint has dried solidly in the tube. My disappointment is replaced with the realisation that I can buy myself a new set. I'd always been stingy with my colours, painting in thin layers so as not to waste excess on the pallet. But that was when I was a student; having a salaried job surely permitted a few extravagances.

I stack up the sketchbooks and canvases and take them through to the living room. Glancing at the clock on the wall I see that it has just gone ten. If I want to go to town, it'd be best to go now before the shops get busy. I quickly check the opening times and location of The Paintery, a three-storied art supply shop Connor had mentioned a few times. The shop is so close to my house, barely a three-minute walk, that I feel tiny bit ashamed that I've never been in when Connor regularly makes an effort to come into town just to browse. I grab my jacket and backpack and head out.

The Paintery is almost overwhelming; the sort of place you either need time to browse and explore, or a list of materials and a familiarity with the layout. Each of the three floors has a different theme: papers, books and canvas on ground floor; paints, mediums, brushes and other tools in the floor below; and an arts and crafts basement. But there is no signage. You either know where you're headed, or you have to ask the staff at the till. I head down to the middle floor of the building and am awestruck by the rows and rows of art supplies. Acrylic paints by chance are on the first aisle, and they are placed next to recommended brushes. I desperately want to touch the bristles on the brushes, but a sign explicitly tells me not to, so I lean in closely trying to imagine how they disperse the paint on the canvas. I feel the surging excitement of inspiration.

"How's it going?" a voice catches me off guard and I jerk away from the brushes.

"Sorry I didn't mean to make you jump," I turn to see a young, slim man wearing a green Paintery apron standing right behind me "I just wanted to see if you needed any help?" his voice is low and his face pleasant. He actually seems keen to help.

"Actually, yes I do please, I just want a nice set of brushes and paints to get started with acrylic," I tell him, and his eyes light up.

"I'd probably recommend something like this," he crouches with a soft click to pull out a box from the bottom shelf. It contains 12 small tubes of paints in a range of colours. The title says 'student quality' which seems fair given my rusty skill set. Then he reaches across to a pouch of four brushes hanging below the single ones. "And these are a good starting point for brushes. Covers most of the basics." He stands, and hands the items to me. He appears pleased with his advice, so I thank him and tuck the goods into the crook of my arm.

"Is there anything else you're looking for?" he asks, seeming keen to continue his quest.

"Oh, maybe a pallet, if you sell them?" I almost smack my jaw for asking such a ridiculous question, but he doesn't seem to notice.

"Sure, just here," he says stretching out the word just as he backs down the aisle to where pallets hang from shelves. "The plastic ones are my favourite as they don't cause the paint to dry out as fast as the wooden," he jostles the frame of his rectangular glasses up his nose as he waits to see which I select. I pick up a long, plastic pallet with dividers for different colours and a hole for the thumb. He nods and says "Nice, I have that one, it's a good weight," as though we are selecting fine jewellery.

I smile and thank him again. He has a wide, genuine smile which seems to be basking in my choices with me. "Anything else?" He splays his empty hands.

"No that's it thanks, just a few bits to get going," I stack the items on top of each other to carry them easier.

"Sweet okay, shall I take these to the cash desk for you?" I allow him to take the pile out of my hands and I follow him to the far end of the shop where a long table is laid out with squares of tissue paper and plastic bags.

"What are you painting?" He asks, matching my pace as we walk; he is about half a foot taller than me, so it takes effort.

"I'm not quite sure, I haven't painted for ages, so I'll probably just have a play," I reply, realising that I hadn't thought that far ahead.

"Excellent, sounds like a good use of a Sunday," he swivels around the cash desk and lays out the goods, then proceeds to wrap them in paper.

"What do you paint?" I ask, realising that he has politely chipped away at the conversation one-sidedly.

"Portraits mainly," he says without looking up "Some on commission, sometimes I do weddings or events, that sort of thing."

"You do weddings?" I check. "How does that work?"

He laughs, and his eyes crinkle in a way that reminds me of Ellen. "Well, I do caricatures at weddings technically. Just really quick watercolours of people. It's more popular than you think!" he exclaims, though there is no defensiveness in his voice "And a good job on the side you know. Good to practice capturing expressions and personalities." He stacks the wrapped items on top of one another and gestures to the plastic bags. "Need a bag?"

"Nah I'll stick them in here," I say, unshouldering my backpack and retrieving my purse. I tap my card to the reader to pay and slide the pile into my bag.

"So, do you have a website?" I ask him, curious to see how good he is.

"Yes!" he tears off my receipt then flips it to the blank side, writes quickly "Timforart dot com," and hands the receipt over. "My email is on there if you have any questions about the paints."

I look at his sunny face and return the grin. "Cheers, that's kind of you. Well, thanks for your help," I drop the receipt into my backpack, zip it back up and sling it back around my shoulder.

"See you later," he says and tucks his hands into the pocket on his immaculate overalls.

I bob my head goodbye and head back to the stairs. The sunshine outside is startling after time in the windowless basement.

Back at the flat I try to think of some ideas to sketch out. The first thing that comes to mind is the ballet. I sit at the table by the window, sketchbook laid out in front of me, and try to shape the figure of one of the dancers on the grainy white sheet. But the slender limbs and tight muscles are impossible to replicate with my unpractised hand. Her body looks flat and static.

I try to fathom how Ellen manages to make a series of numbers look and feel so human. There must be some elements your mind fills in, there's no way she'd have time to develop such intricate details. My hand idles away layering shadow on the limbs, and I realise that I have disengaged. The new paints and brushes feel more exciting, perhaps I should crack on with them without an underpinning sketch.

I retrieve my bag and unpack The Paintery items. Suddenly I wonder whether I've forgotten the medium you need to wash the brushes, then retract this thought, convinced it's actually oil paints. I am reminded of how out of touch I have become with the process. How each step used to make perfect sense, but now I am struggling to remember if you can use water to dilute the paints. I resign to googling the answers to my questions on my laptop but get sucked into a series of videos about painting tips and techniques.

None of my paint tubes are even open, but an hour passes whilst I prepare myself online. Eventually the videos take me on a complete tangent, and I remember that I had plans to actually paint today. I cast around my brain for some inspiration, then flick through my old sketchbooks. Halfway through I come across some crude sketches of lean Egon Schiele models. Their waif-like figures and grotesque features weirdly alluring. I remember a painting I had seen years back at a Klimt exhibition in Liverpool of Schiele and Klimt together, dark and entwined. Unable to recall the name, I plug terms into my search bar until I find it. The Hermits. The murky geometry and striking expressions kindle inspiration in me and I sketch out a vague outline of the two figures in the middle of my canvas.

Twisting each of the paint tubes open, I push a couple of inches from each onto the pallet. Next, I open the pack of brushes, and withdraw a flat headed one around an inch wide. With this brush, I pat some of the colours together, testing the blends they can make; attempting to replicate the spectrum of dark colours in the painting. At first, I am sparse and a light touch with the paints, but as I relax more into the repetition of loading paint onto the brush and transferring to the canvas, I become more generous. Soon the canvas fills with shadowy colours. The faces still stark white and untouched by the wide brush.

When the background is sufficiently filled with colourful shapes, and the foreground coalesces in the shadows of the figures, I contemplate the faces and their expressions. I am put off by the sinister looks in the original, so aim for softer, lighter faces. In the end, I spend more time laying down and overwriting the faces, moving further away from the harsh angles into rounded faces. Happy eventually with their mellow expressions, I consider hair. I feel that blonde and red will contrast best against dark background, and layer on hair in thick strands.

After a few minutes leaning in close to the painting, and leaning back to view it as a whole, I decide to take a break, my stomach turning in hunger. Snapped out of my concentration, I realise how quiet my flat is. Not even the sound of neighbours or traffic. I plug my phone into portable speakers in the kitchen and select my current favourite playlist. The jangly piano intro to *This Year* by The Mountain Goats fills the space and I put a couple of pittas in the toaster, then chop up some carrots and sugar snap peas to scoop up humous for a late lunch plate. I tip out the morning's coffee grinds and put another pot on the stove, listening to the lyrics of the song and getting a strong urge to drive somewhere. Unlike my friends who live outside of the city, I don't have the need or space for a car, so have thus far got by on my Dutch bike and public transport. Perhaps I will rent a car and take myself on a driving holiday this year, drive up to Scotland and finally see the famous scenery, wind around small towns and stay in bed and breakfasts, bag some munros and hike around lochs.

The pittas pop from the toaster and I slice them into dipping sticks and take my plate to the living space. I flick on the TV and navigate to a documentary I had saved about Women's prisons. My mind only half engaged in the story as I eat and start to think about Ellen, whether she is working on my scenario and whether she might text me.

12

The next five days of work slide in and out of view. A blur of long hours at the computer, adjusting parameters and percentages to see where areas of significant activity lay on maps of my participants' brains. By Friday, I start mentally preparing for an evening with Riya at the Vie Lab. I had text her earlier in the week to check she'd cleared my attendance with Ellen, I didn't fancy another cold reception, but was reassured that it was fine, especially given that I was 'teacher's pet'.

At 5pm I power down my machine and bolt from campus. If I hurry, I'll have an hour back at my flat before I need to set off for the lab. My stomach is jittery with nerves; I imagine that, again, dinner will have to wait until after the session.

Back at the flat, I eye the clock and decide I have time to shower and freshen up. Even though I know I'm not in on the session, I feel an urge to make a good impression. I cycle through my *extra-effort routine* of exfoliating, shaving, and conditioning my body. Then out of the shower, I brush, floss and whiten my teeth. A little foundation, mascara and tinted lip balm warms up my face. I debate texting Riya to ask what she is wearing, but I know this will offer me little solace from my preparatory nerves. She always manages to look put together and smart, and my wardrobe has very little content to compare. I pull on jeans and a top with buttons from throat to sternum, which I recall is absurdly called a grandad collar. The outfit makes me feel comfortably confident; the top clings nicely to the areas I want it to and relaxes around the areas I like it to. I glance at myself in the mirror and wonder whether Riya will notice the extra effort I've made and take the piss.

With twenty minutes until I need to leave, I wake up my laptop and open one of my social feeds, scrolling absently through the photos and words. There are four messages in my inbox, I open them. Group chats line up on the screen, each thread indicating that I am way behind in the conversation. I read back through some of the recent messages and offer non-committal points and suggestions towards future meet ups. All scheduled for months down the line, when people assume they will have more time and/or money. After replying, I feel oddly drained. Like I have fast forwarded through a crowd of conversations and absorbed too much.

It occurs to me that I could try arriving a little early and speak to Ellen before Riya gets there and as though sensing my plan, Riya texts "Heading into town now, so excited! x". I reply to say I too am on my way and the nerves in my arms start to tingle.

As I pull the door to my building closed, I see a silver sports car hastily pull up on the pavement ahead. A stream of insults about parking on double yellow lines ping into my head but then I recognise that it is Connor's car. He winds down the window and leans over the empty passenger seat waving. In his sharp business suit with slick combed hair, he barely looks like the guy I danced sweatily with at the weekend.

"Good timing, I'm just stopping on the way home from work to give you this Virginial Howl book," he grins, reaches into the back seat and presents a large hardback book. I completely forgot that he said he would drop the book around this week. "I was going to park up and knock but looks like you're heading out."

I thank him for the book, and catch him scanning my face, acknowledging the makeup.

"So, you look nice, where are you off?" he says with a sly smile.

I fumble for a moment, trying to think of the fastest way to escape small talk. "I've got a date in town," I lie hastily, straightening away from the window to hide my reddening face. "I'm actually a little late or I would stop and chat."

"Oh, jump in and I'll give you a ride into town," Connor exclaims, opening the passenger door, "and you can fill me in."

I panic, considering the imaginary details I'd have to spin up on the spot.

"Thanks, but don't worry about it, we'd get stuck in the Friday rush hour heading into town. I might as well walk." I try a sweet smile to stifle my rising impatience, but he seems slightly put out that I declined his offer.

"Okay sure, but we need to have dinner soon to discuss this secret dating life you've got going on." He closes the door, then through the window exclaims, 'Wait, is this that woman from work you mentioned? Is it?" His voice creaks with excitement.

I try to present a coy smile, but nerves twitch my mouth peculiarly. "I'll tell you everything if it goes well."

"Well, have fun and stay safe," he winks. "Text me tonight please." Then he winds up the window and wave him off.

I feel weird lying to Connor, but I am not in any position to tell him the truth. Besides I am as nervous as if I was going on a date, so that's almost a half truth? I debate jogging back up the three flights of stairs to drop the book in my flat, then realise that would make me late so I carry the massive book under my arm as I power walk into town.

Riya and I arrive at Ryan's Bookbinding at the same time. I briefly explain about running into Connor and loaning his Virginia Howl book.

"I thought you'd brought some reading in case my scenario was boring," Riya chuckles. She presses the buzzer and after a pause Ellen's voice announces the shop-closed spiel. I get an excited tingle when I hear her voice and look to Riya, who is beaming too.

We skip up the stairs to the reception room and Ellen is at the desk to greet us. She is wearing a light blue plain dress, her short hair clipped back from her face revealing a soft, round jawline. I feel half-drunk trying not to seem giddy.

"Good evening, ladies," she says, politely "Riya told me you planned to join us again this evening Nicole. Glad you could make it." Ellen directs the welcome towards me, but her receptionist manner is just as chilled as the first time I arrived with Riya. I had hoped that visiting her house might have warmed her up to me.

Without further pleasantries, we are guided through to the control room. I start to feel the twisted combination of excitement and trepidation. Riya, though, is clearly leaning towards the excitement end of the spectrum, grinning widely. The monitors in the control room are already set up and ready to go.

"The last client had a short session, so I had more time to setup," Ellen explains. I secretly curse Connor for intercepting my journey, I definitely could have snuck in an extra five minutes.

"Perfect!" Riya clasps her hands together. "Should I go straight in then?"

"You can do, just leave your personal effects out here please," Ellen replies, turning her attention to the computers.

Riya stacks her bag and jacket on the chair by the door, casts a wide smile at me, then enters the white room. Ellen tucks her chair in towards the screens. I position myself to the left of her again. She doesn't acknowledge my presence as she busies herself typing. Her frostiness touches me in a way I can't quite grasp. It is unusual to drink wine casually at someone's house, then within a week rebuild a completely professional barrier. I fix my face into passive nonchalance in case she looks my way, but my thoughts are racing. I try to focus on Riya rocking on the balls of her feet in the lab.

Ellen leans over, bringing a warm scent of rosy washing powder with her, and informs Riya of the usual procedures via the intercom. I interlace my fingers and slide them between my knees, trying not to let the anticipation overwhelm me. The lights flicker off then back on, and Ellen silently hands me the headpiece to put on. I affix the band and look through the window and see that the Vie Lab now resembles a sparsely furnished bedroom; a large four poster bed, two chairs and a chest of drawers all arranged neatly like a showroom. Riya is perched on the edge of the bed, her posture awkward but her face gleeful.

Without further ado, the door at the far end of the room opens and three tall men in business attire enter, each of them carrying a briefcase. Two of them take a seat in the chairs next to the bed, and the third stands next to the chest of drawers; here he opens his briefcase and, in an almost comical way, pulls out metres and metres of red ribbon. The other two men watch on as he approaches the bed with the fabric. He smiles, a slightly unhinged edge to the expression. Riya's face drops out of its grin.

The man with the ribbon leans in towards Riya, lifts her top up over her head and drops it to the floor. Folding his arms and casting an appraising glance over her scantily covered breasts, he's commands her to, "Take everything else off." Riya obliges.

I look over to Ellen in the dark and her slightly hunched silhouette, tapping furiously at the keyboard. I wonder how many different sexual scenarios she has written. A man's voice in the room groans "See what you have done to me." I have no desire to know what has been done; I feel a strange detachment to the scenario playing out.

I shift a little closer to Ellen, "Did you write this, or did Riya? I ask, the first question that comes to mind. Ellen clacks three more keys, then swivels in her chair, looking at me for the first time since we'd sat down.

"Mostly Riya. Though some of her ideas got a bit mixed together so I did some tidying up." Then, after a beat, she lowers her voice to say, "Well to be honest, this scenario is mainly just a hash together of various other code with a few edits," Ellen laughs. "Don't tell Riya!" In the dim light of the room, I see that the corners of her mouth have turned up slightly, conspiratorially.

As the four-way businessman orgy hammers on in my periphery, I try desperately to think of anything else that might keep Ellen talking.

"Can you tell me what each of the terminals is for?" I ask quickly, sensing that she is about to turn back to work again.

Ellen indicates to the screen closest to me "That first one is monitoring the conditions in the room," nodding into the room where Riya is writhing "second one is the interface between the room and the machine, the third one here is the input terminal for the code - basically where the scenario is derived from. The last one back there is access to the database." Her attention snaps back to the scenario terminal, tracking the code and glancing into the room, presumably to check it matched up. I sensed I should be quiet for a while and let Ellen work.

Back in the room, a kneeling businessman is opening the box and removing a thumb sized silver bullet. It is unclear from my viewpoint where this gets inserted, but Riya seems to enjoy it.

I start to think about the complexity of the situation and how many different overlapping events are occurring, each responsive to the other. I want to ask Ellen about it but get the impression that she is busy orchestrating, so I allow my gaze to drift back to the room where things are getting frantic. Riya orgasms forcefully, setting off a chain reaction amongst the other men.

A jarring silence follows, with the men hitching up their trousers, and Riya being unravelled from the ribbon in a seemingly automated routine. As the men breeze out of the door, Riya is still lying flat out on the bed. Her face sweaty and hair tangled.

Ellen leans over to the microphone again "Hi Riya, we'll give you a few minutes to dress then reset the room, if that's OK?" Riya nods, drained.

Leaning back into her chair Ellen folds her arms and lets out a small nasal laugh "That can be surprisingly knackering," she says.

I leap on the break from professionalism:

"Are you speaking from experience?"

"You could say that," she replies laughing a little louder. Twisting back to the computer, her hands hovering over the keyboard, waiting to answer queries on the screen as they arrive. It occurs to me, with an odd feeling of awe, that she probably tries out most of the scenarios herself; if nothing else than to make sure they were suitable and safe.

Riya has managed to sit up in the room and is dragging clothes back onto her spent body. I decide to chance it with one last brazen question before reality resumes:

"So, are you planning to wear me out like that?" I ask.

"Ohh, I've got something quite different in mind for you," Ellen says, flicking the lights off in the Lab. Her expression unreadable in the momentary darkness.

13

Once outside Riya starts to complain about her car being in the garage, and her legs being wobbly. The night is still light and warm, so I anticipate a stroll and chat, but she hails a taxi as soon as we get to the main road. I jump in too, planning to press for details, but Riya sits quietly in the cab with her eyes closed dramatically, clearly avoiding my questions. So, I stare out of the window at the Friday night energy of people weaving in and out of bars and restaurants, and in no time, we are outside my flat. I have to jostle Riya awake to give her some cash. The taxi driver looks at her in his rear-view mirror, weighing up whether he should turf her out with me.

"She's not drunk," I tell him, "She's just knackered from working late."

Riya smirks and closes her eyes again, folding her arms across her chest.

Back in the flat I feel voraciously hungry. The first time I've felt hungry all day. Excitement had propelled me past two meals and now I am ravished with the comedown. The clock in the kitchen shows 21:09, took late to bother cooking, so I pull out my phone to order something that can by cycled to my door. Amidst the stack of notifications on the home screen, one immediately stands out. A text message from Ellen. It catches me off guard, I hadn't expected to hear for her until my next session. My phone seems to slow down as I try to open the message as quickly as possible. It reads:

"I'm keen to test out the scenario I've built for you now. Can you make an out of hours' appointment this weekend?"

The sickening excitement I only just quelled rushes back in full force. I resist the urge to type "Yes fucking please." Propped up against the kitchen counter, I draft and redraft a response. Each time trying to suffocate my enthusiasm.

Finally, I settle for "That'd be great! What day works best for you?"

The minute I send it, I recoil in the wording choice. Too business casual, but too late to change. So, I browse the local food chains for the shortest delivery timed meals to override my stream of thoughts. One bento box will be with me in fifteen minutes. I put a bottle of wine in the fridge to chill a little and wonder whether it is inappropriate to change into pyjamas even though the delivery was only minutes away. No, of course it isn't, this is the whole point of ordering food to your house, you can do whatever you please. I change into light cotton trousers and a matching t-shirt, pulling a loose hoody over the top so I don't startle anyone with my unbridled breasts.

I turn my phone notifications onto loud under the guise that I could hear any food delivery updates but really it is so I will notice Ellen's reply as it arrives. Whilst I wait, I browse films trying to find something engrossing to take my mind off the evening's events. A twisting excitement still writhes in my stomach.

My phone judders loudly on the coffee table and I reach over immediately.

"Tomorrow at 5pm?" the message shows in full on the lock screen. Casual, non-committal, breezy. Her previous message felt steeped in meaning, yet this one is back to professional calendar invitations. I don't know what I'd expected, but my mood deflates slightly. Whilst I mentally toss around different scenarios in which Ellen has also overthought her response to me, the buzzer on the wall sounds and I jump to my feet.

An athletic-looking, young man with a bike helmet under his arm fetches my box up the stairs and to my door. I wonder whether he is a student at the University, and instantly regret answering the door in my pyjamas. I try to position my arms in the most breast-minimising way as I exchange food for money, but he doesn't seem to notice, jogging on to his next delivery with barely a glance at my face.

The wine has a nice chill now, so I pour a glass and carry with the food to the sofa. My phone still sits on the coffee table, I know I will have to reply to Ellen before I can relax.

"Perfect, see you there," I add a smiley face at the end of the message to try and unknot us from the ties of business communications, but I instantly regret it. I debate texting Riya to tell her about my secret appointment, but part of me wants to keep it to myself. Imagining that I am Ellen's secret favourite gives me a weird buoyancy, and I do not wish to hear anything that would suggest otherwise. To avoid any further temptations or debates, I turn off my phone and direct my energies to pinching noodles into my mouth.

◆◆◆

Later, in that weird, contemplative, semi-conscious state of falling asleep, I replay the session with Riya in my mind. I wonder whether all of her sessions are sexual, and why she would want me to be there to see them. Is there a deeper element than voyeurism in inviting me? I run through the options: one where Riya is a sexual exhibitionist, my primary hypothesis; another where Riya simply enjoys flaunting her invitation to the project, an unlikely but not inconceivable idea; and a third where Riya spotted a potential match between me and Ellen and has brought us together, my wildcard scenario.

I need to make time to speak to Riya about everything, in person, with wine.

14

It's hard to sleep after the salty dinner and wine, and I wake every few hours to try and quench an urgent thirst. Yet, I still rise early, wired as though two espressos into the day. Too many hours stretch between now and the appointment, so I try to fall back to sleep. Then, failing this, try to rest myself into some kind of meditation. My overactive brain prevents this from happening, so I retrieve my tablet from the dressing table and flick through some social feeds for a while.

Just as I am about to doze off again, I remember the Virginia Howl book that Connor loaned me. The flat feels quiet and tidy, the sort of orderliness I am not prepared for yet, so I tiptoe quickly past the windows in my pyjamas to retrieve the book, bringing it back to the dishevelled bedroom. I open the bedroom curtains widely, and the bright morning light streams in, filling the room with a leisurely glow. I climb back into bed and crack the book open across my knees.

The introduction gives a detailed, if slightly over-analytical account of Howl's life. How she was the granddaughter of the famous philosopher Jerome Howl, a man who's work I had little time or respect for given its misogynistic overtones. I skim over Howl's history and pause to read the last couple of paragraphs in more detail, bemused by the book describing her painting style as "juxtaposing the conscious and subconscious," which is almost without meaning in the psychological sense of the words. Nevertheless, I leaf through the pages, seeking examples of this theory in her art.

Howl's paintings are captivating to see in full colour prints and I imagine they are more powerful in real life. The expressions on her subjects' faces are emotive, yet many of the postures relaxed and languid. I turn the pages in idle appreciation of the beauty, each page revealing another person and their warped expression. About halfway through the book, I turn the page and a shiver shoots down my spine. A ghostly, wide-eyed woman stares out at me, bearing a striking resemblance to Ellen. Short, blonde hair in an exaggerated parting, thin skin with a slight blue hue, and impassive, almost cold expression on her face. I find it intoxicating looking at her powerful, nonchalant face and am compelled to image search what the model had looked like in person. Disappointingly, she does not resemble Ellen when captured in photography. But the itch does not feel scratched yet. I look at the picture for a good while until an idea unfolds. Sliding out of bed onto the floor I pull open my chest of drawers; underneath the stacks of paper and pencils I dig out a piece of canvas board just larger than A3 and carry it through to the living room with a handful of pencils. I will dress, and then I will paint.

Wearing old jogging trousers and an oversized band T-shirt from my teens, I sit myself on the living room with the Howl book in front of me. I start to wish I had an easel to prop the canvas board on, but my knees will suffice. I set about sketching; half drawing the woman from the book, half imagining the features of Ellen. After half an hour of sketching and cursing the lack of erasers in my collection of art supplies, I feel the draft of my woman is close enough. The paints too had been returned to the chest of drawers when I had tidied the flat, so I stretch out my limbs and collect the set, brushes and pallet, bringing them through to the living room with a jar of water. I connect my phone to the speakers in the kitchen and scroll to CocoRosie's *La Maison de Mon Reve*, an album that rekindles memories of studying, painting and drifting around campus at university. The jarring intro song, oddly relaxing through its familiarity.

With my feet tucked beneath the opposite knee, I dab paint onto the canvas for a long time, desperately trying to recreate the surreal blur Howl casts on her subjects. After a full album's worth of painting, I start to feel that even a vague resemblance to a human face would suffice. Though some of the brush strokes feel natural and easy, others take time to conjure the hand-eye coordination I once had. Edges and contours look a little sloppy. The base coat is finished as the music jumps forwards three years to *The Adventures of Ghosthorse and Stillborn*. My buttocks start to feel numb pressed against wooden floor, so I uncurl myself and lay the canvas on the table to dry whilst I stretch out. A grumble releases from my stomach as I stand, and I realise that I haven't eaten breakfast yet. My phone tells me that it's almost noon, so I opt for a brunch of poached eggs on toast with a cup of tea, Earl Grey, hot. As I sit by the window and dig in, I feel a warm satisfaction knowing that the next layer of painting will take me a step closer to the finished picture, and closer to my out of hours session with Ellen.

◆ ◆ ◆

Afternoon slowly turns into evening and the anticipation starts to creep in. I run through my preparations at home; showering, perking up my face and picking out my least creased jeans and t-shirt. Despite the overwhelming urge to forecast a plan of the evening, I try to focus my energies on short term tasks like tying my shoes, locking the front door and bounding down the steps to the lobby. I plug myself into the music on my phone and attempt to pace myself walking across town, trying not to build up a sweat.

I turn onto the alleyway a little early but press the button anyway. Ellen buzzes me in, and I mentally count the twenty-six stairs leading to the landing, pocketing and un-pocketing my phone nervously. As I turn in to the bright reception room, I see Ellen standing in her usual spot behind the desk but am surprised to see her wearing unusually casual clothes, black leggings with a loose fit dress. Her short, blonde hair pulled back into a tiny bun.

"Please excuse the mess, "Ellen says, casting a look around the room which appears to me to be largely the same, but with the addition of a vacuum cleaner. "I'm in the middle of cleaning the place."

I hadn't anticipated this, and it throws me off kilter. "Don't you have a cleaner?" I ask.

Ellen laughs without humour:

"Ha, no!" she peels off rubber gloves and rolls her eyes. "We're lacking both funds and trust for any external support, so we – well, I - end up doing it."

The money comment makes me wince given that I essentially have a free pass to the theme park.

"Why don't you start charging for sessions?" I ask. "People would pay good money for this experience!"

"That's the long-term aim," Ellen says, bending to file away some loose papers, "but we need to finish beta phase testing and get a few other things sorted first. We're intentionally flying under the radar at the moment." She straightens and fixes a straight look at me "Setting the Vie Lab up as a private, tax-paying business will start all sorts of inquiries."

This intrigues and unsettles me. The back-alleyway secret lab perception starts to ring true. What if none of the equipment is legitimate, or even safe?

"Do you and the Professor take it in turns to run shifts?" I ask, sensing that this isn't the case, seeing an opportunity to break down the barriers.

Ellen turns on her heels and walks through to the control room, encouraging me to follow by answering. "Not anymore, he's too busy attending conferences." There are bitter overtones in her voice, and I wonder if she will elaborate, but she doesn't. Instead, her face suddenly shifts into a wide smile.

"Right well I've got a bit of a surprise for you," my heart flutters as she leans over the machine and starts the login process. "It's an idea I've been working on for a little while. Sort of a pet project." All of my excitement rushes uneasily to my gut as I process the idea of a novel concept in an experimental programme.

"I really hope you like it. But remember if you are uncomfortable at any time, I can stop everything immediately." She turns back to me, the glint in her eyes makes me want to like it.

"Sounds cool," I try to pitch my voice to sound enthusiastic.

"Do you want to head through then?" Ellen asks. I oblige; every muscle in my body requiring coercion to walk *casually* over the threshold.

Before I have time to acclimatise, the lights dim and the blood runs cold to my feet. After a stretch, they flick back on, but my eyes take a while to adjust. I realise that Ellen hasn't spoken to me via the voiceover and the disconnect is unsettling. I glance back to the door, but it has disappeared. Dark shadows engulf most of the space around me, but two spotlights are illuminating patches on a small wooden stage in the centre of the room. As I approach the lights, I see that behind the stage is a heavy black curtain, which comes into view only as it swishes gently. I stand at the edge of the stage, the only spectator, and wait. In the silence of the room, I can hear the blood surge in my ears and try to tune out of the sound. It's easy to spiral into anxiety when you become aware of your amplified heart rate.

Suddenly, a chorus of string instruments erupt from the surrounding. I twist my head around to source the sound, but it seems to be coming from everywhere, and nowhere. Then the black curtain is drawn apart by two pale arms. A small, slender woman leads a man with a similar physique onto the stage. The two of them have remarkably similar, bodies, but their skin contrasts warm and cool tones. Both wear matching white tights, leotards and pumps; both have delicate, smooth

89

faces. As they move closely, in synchrony, it is hard to tell them apart.

The dancers exude chemistry as they move, running their hands along one another's limbs. The fluidity of their dancing is intoxicating to watch; they work in unison to curl and uncurl their bodies. Their expressions are neutral, but their movements urgent, undulating. They stand momentarily embraced in a kiss, then pull slowly away. I feel the ripple of excitement I had experienced in the theatre.

The man turns and the woman slides behind him, her torso obscured by his but her hands snake around to caresses his abdomen. She slides her palms up to his chest, across his throat, then back down towards his midriff, and then further down still. Suddenly, and almost cruelty, the hands withdraw back into the darkness. The man's eyes snap open and he looks directly at me, acknowledging my presence for the first time. It hadn't occurred to me that they could see me, I had assumed the anonymity of an audience member at a show and feel embarrassed by my secret arousal.

The dancer steps towards me and extends his hand. I am frozen briefly, then almost out of obligation, lean into the light and take hold of his soft fingers. The spotlight feels too revealing, yet the visible area seems very small. He leads me on stage, and I feel stiff moving alongside his relaxed poise. His hands draw along the outline of my arms and I notice that his hands are the same temperature as my own skin. He twists me away and brings the heat of his body against my back; his hands are gentle in their choreographed exploration of my body.

When the feeling becomes almost intolerably provocative, he pauses and turns my hips towards him. Except that I am now looking at the face of the woman; the man is nowhere to be seen. I cannot recall the two switching places; I certainly didn't notice a break in contact. As if to quieten the questions on my lips, she leans in and kisses me softly. It feels familiar, as though we had kissed before and I find myself running my hands up through her hair, pulling her closer, encouraging her. Then she is pulling away and I open my eyes to see that it is the man who faces me now. I start to question the switch; had I imagined the woman? Well, of course I *imagined* her. The man steps closer and I can feel the warmth of his torso, a breath away from me. We kiss and it overlaps with the memory of the prior.

I lose myself in the moment; his hands hot against my skin and mine pressing into the smooth muscle of his back. The string music continues a fevered tempo and I feel intoxicated, passionate. I want more.

But then then the music draws to an abrupt close and the dancer slips out of my embrace. Before I can comprehend the absence, they have retreated into the shadows of the curtains. My hands pull back to my own body, clasping arms in defence. The stage feels oppressive in its emptiness.

I wait, expecting Ellen's voice to emerge from the hidden speaker, but nothing comes. The silence rings around my thudding heartbeat.

"End game," I whisper into the void, and after a brief pause the lights flick off.

15

Ellen swings around in her chair when I re-enter the control room, a jarring return to normality.

"So, what did you think?" she asks, leaning back and raising her eyebrows.

"Erm yeah, very interesting," I say, wondering how much truth to reveal, "Not quite what I expected, but I enjoyed it."

Ellen swivels the chair gently side to side, rocking on her toes. "Interesting, good. Okay so what did you think of the body switching element? That's new."

"Yes, that was unique," I scrabble for better words, "Like nothing I've ever encountered before," a blush starts to creep up my neck. I've never had a sexual debrief before, but Ellen seems unfazed. It's all business to her.

"That's what I was thinking, you know cross some boundaries but keep it light," she smiles and plants her feet on the ground. I think she senses my awkwardness, her smile fading back to professional, so I quickly blurt out: "It's exciting!"

Ellen nods, encouraging further elaboration, so I continue, "But I am not a fan of the disappearing at the end. It gave me a weird empty feeling." I surprise myself saying this, I hadn't planned to.

"Ah sorry, that was an oversight on my behalf," Ellen says, standing up. "I was so excited about you doing the trial that I didn't finish coding the outro. That was something that got picked up in early trials actually, people wanted to it to seem like the characters came from somewhere, had somewhere to go. To feel like they are more permanent." She laughs and shrugs. "Doesn't matter either way in reality."

I was unsettled to think of Ellen omitting something from a scenario. When you're in the Vie Lab, you assign a lot of trust to the programme, and it's easy to forget that human error might be present in the input. I want to ask more questions, but Ellen starts to walk back through to the reception. I follow, racking my brain for some conversational thread to pick back up with.

"What are you doing for dinner?" I ask quickly, before I overthink it.

"Dinner?" she sounds the word out like a foreign language. Then her eyes turn soft and apologetic. "Sorry, I just ate a sandwich whilst you were in the lab, I knew I'd be here late." I can't tell if she's sorry she ate whilst working, or if she feels bad rejecting my poorly concealed suggestion. I deflect the conversation to show neither issues bother me.

"What else have you got to do tonight then?"

Ellen slides behind the reception desk and taps the computer awake.

"Just boring admin stuff." I can see her attention is drifting back to work. "Sometimes I come in on the weekend to catch up. It's not too arduous. And hopefully I won't be doing it for much longer."

"Are you thinking of leaving?" I ask, tamping down rising panic.

"Oh no, god no!" she laughs "Could you imagine me working in a legitimate workplace? I'd have to learn how to do small talk."

"Urgh, the world doesn't need another weather conversationist." I smile, trying to seem casual as I ask, "Are you going to employ someone to help out then?"

"Yeah, I think that's the plan." Ellen raises her eyebrows. "Why, are you volunteering?"

"Well, I've already got my dream job," I say, less conviction in my voice than I planned. "But I am definitely keen to help out in my free time. I suppose some of it could be classed as CPD?"

"CPD?" Ellen shakes her head, "See, more workplace nonsense I'd have to get into." She types a few characters into the computer, then sidles back around the desk and heads to the exit. This is clearly my cue to leave, so I follow her to the exit.

At the door, she steps towards me, crossing a personal space boundary, and for a fleeting moment, I wonder if she is going to kiss me. Instead, she says: "I'd really like to hear any other ideas you have."

I look down at her, the angle a little awkward, and say, "Sure."

She takes a step back as though realising the proximity. "Well drop me a text if you think of anything." She leads back to the reception desk. I am transfixed for a moment, wondering if I have overlooked a glaring opportunity. I nod and exit, desperate for fresh air.

16

I wake early on Sunday morning feeling invigorated, and oddly aroused. I try to recall the dream I was having but as soon as I probe, the scenario slips away into the darkness. Instead, hazy images of Ellen come to mind, sitting in the control room, busy with the computer screens. And I approach her, gently touching her shoulders, leaning over to kiss her exposed skin on her neck. In bed, my fingers slide beneath my shorts.

Rolling onto my side, I lie still and let my heart rate settle, enjoying the heavy pleasure of my limbs. I start to wonder about what other people do to build up a powerful orgasm. I reach for my tablet. The search generates some suggestions that I've already heard of, tantric sex, controlled breathing etcetera, but as my eyes skim the results, I come across something I've never seen before *pleasure torture*. The idea startles and intrigues me. I click it.

The link takes me to a website of video clips with men and women wearing blindfolds, tied to beds or belted to tables. It looks like S&M, something I've never been particularly interested in, but mid-scroll I see something that jumps out at me. I maximise the thumbnail and the video start to play - a blindfolded woman is lying on an observation table, her limbs shackled to the four corners. Three men work on her naked body. They are orchestrating her pleasure, building her up to the tipping point, then removing the devices. Her body writhes with the sudden absence of stimulation. When she is still, the vibration is applied again. I note that the video is over thirty minutes long. The tingle of arousal creeps back; I want Ellen to write a pleasure torture scenario for me.

I pick up my phone to text Ellen, then pause. I can't bring myself to write the words *pleasure torture*, but now I've got the idea in my head I need to vent it, release the pressure.

"I've had another Vie Lab idea," I type and send to Ellen. I feel bold and excited, but as soon as the message leaves the safety of my phone, regret starts to rise like bile in my throat. I wait two minutes then get out of bed.

The ping of a message. I snatch my phone. "That was quick! What is it?" Ellen replies. I feel elated at the fast response, pleased with myself for taking the risk.

"Heard of restricted orgasms?" I ask, sending before I reword, overthink and lose the moment.

A five-minute, painful interlude of me clenching and unclenching my hands, debating breakfast then flitting back to the screen. Then:

"Sure, what's your scenario?" a typically nonchalant response.

"I was hoping you might help with that," I reply, hoping I seem playful rather than incompetent.

"No problem, I'll get on it," Ellen sends back instantly. I feel deflating by her detached professionalism, but then a second message pops up; a winking face.

And I am in agony.

17

On Monday, I arrive at work just after 9am. The offices on my corridor are empty and the patting noise my shoes make on the linoleum reverberates in the silence. I feel the day stretching out before me, long and dull. I've never really thought about how much energy other people bring to the day.

I log in to my email account and the server delivers a handful of messages. Most are mass mails for the whole University staff, funding updates and summer events on campus. I check the project calendar to see if any work is due this week. Nothing. It was looking to be an exceptionally quiet week. My barren calendar reminds me that I have a stack of holiday leave to use up, so I draft an email to the head of department requesting the rest of the week off. In the time it takes me to brew a cup of tea, she replies encouraging me to make the most of the holiday. We all know there's little point killing time in the office when there are no results to analyse or students to placate. Some of my colleagues relish the quiet of summer; finally settling into their passion projects and catching up on correspondence with international researchers. Last year I had a pet project to work on: firing off publications from my PhD, but this year I haven't had anything with strong enough data.

I text Riya to ask about lunch plans. She confirms that she can meet as usual and is excited to tell me about her date at the weekend. I hold off on probing via text because I'd prefer the story in person. My own dating life had been dry since I settled into a job. I lost interest in the extracurricular hobbies I had done as a post-grad. And with it, I inadvertently lost the circles of acquaintances I once had. It's funny how you take for granted the casual dates you get through groups of people. I'd settled into Manchester life; making friends in the department, getting closer to Riya, and keeping in contact with Connor who conveniently worked in Manchester too. My circle of friends had drawn tighter, which I enjoyed, but it did make for less fresh faces.

There's a loud knock at the door and I nearly jump out of my chair. It's been so long since anyone stopped by, I had almost forgotten I was at work. I glance around to see who it is.

"Oh come in." I tell Jonathan, the computer technician hovering on the other side of the glass.

"Sorry to interrupt you Dr Harris, I wondered if you wanted me to get started on your online learning portal for next term?" He asks, poking only his head around the door to avoid crowding the small office "I'd need an overview of your module content today."

Ah shit, I had completely forgotten we were making our lecture content available online now.

"Sure, no problem," I tell him, hoping it's not obvious that this had slipped my mind "I'll email you the plan after lunch. Thanks for the reminder!"

He closes the door quietly and shuffles away down the corridor. I am glad of a deadline to work to, so the day doesn't drag.

◆ ◆ ◆

I bump into Riya on the walk over to The Coffee Shop and we have a quick moan about the last-minute online learning upload, she has also just been reminded by Jonathan. We pick out sandwiches and coffees on autopilot, ramble about work, then find a table near the window.

"So, tell me your date news. Is it the same guy as last week?" I ask, keen for stories that might invigorate my boring day.

"Welllll," she draws the word out, enjoying the drama. "No, it's someone new. His name is Sal, he works in structural engineering and he's really nice." Riya looks up to see what my initial reaction is, but I don't have enough information to react to so take a bite of my halloumi wrap. She continues "We bonded over our shared interest in Coen brothers' films. Went to see the new one at the weekend, then out for dinner to talk about it."

"Oh yeah. Just dinner and film? How very 1950s of you." I raise one eyebrow, which I know she enjoys. Riya laughs loudly. Her readiness to laugh always tickles me.

"OK yeah, I invited him back to my place after dinner. I had to check that I *really* liked him, you know." Riya plays coy, but I know she fully enjoys the mild scandal.

"And did you, *really* like him?" I ask with such implication in my voice that Riya giggles again.

"Yes, very much so," she finally takes a bite of her sandwich. "He stayed for ages on Sunday morning, and we've been texting loads since. I feel like I'm a teenager again."

She pulls out her phone to show me his online profile; a series of photos of a handsome man in his early thirties illustrating his interests - standing on a mountain top in full hiking gear, holding a drink mid-cheers at dinner, in a group of friends on a night out. He seems like a nice enough guy, and I tell her so.

"Seriously though Nicole you should try this app it's quite fun." I pretend like I'm interested in her describing details, but I don't have any intention of joining. I feel I am already, secretly, pursuing new realms of sexual exploration.

18

On my first day of annual leave, the alarm goes off early because I forgot to disable it. I still feel sleepy so allow myself to drift off again. In this semi-conscious state, I dream about being Ellen's lab assistant. Half imagining the scenarios, half letting my brain unspool the situation. By the time I am fully awake, I've convinced myself that Ellen could actually want me as a lab assistant. I debate asking the question. Surely no harm in offering.

I pick up my phone, wipe away the updates and open the conversation with Ellen. A wave of adrenaline hinders my trail of thought. I never know how to pitch texts to her. After padding out, and clipping down a message, I send:

"Hey, I have some time off work this week if you need any help around the lab?" I try to imagine texting my old PhD lab partner Graham, keeping it light and non-committal.

To take my mind of the weight of pressure on the reply, I shower, dress and start making eggs for breakfast. Just as I lay out my plate for toast, I hear my phone jangle in the other room. I finish plating up my breakfast, resisting the urge to dive straight at my phone, saving face from no-one, but trying to seem calm to myself. I even crack some salt and pepper over the eggs to delay the inevitable. Then I finally allow myself to reach for my phone. Ellen has replied:

"Hey, I'm not in the lab until tomorrow. But I work on scenarios at home if you want to pop round this afternoon? I'll be in from about 3pm."

Another invitation to her house! And the potential to see how she spins words into virtual reality. I force myself to eat breakfast before I reply, giddy about the prospect. I tell her I'll head over around 3pm, trying to sound breezy. Five hours to kill.

I wonder whether to do some research, but as soon as I open my laptop, I get stuck on what to search. Should I try to brush up on neuroimaging? I feel like I have more to learn from Ellen than the internet I open a private browser and try to find the pleasure torture scenario I had been inspired by the other day. A few pages into searching, I find the video. Now on a larger screen I try to get a closer look at the vibrator they use. I realise I have never seen anything like it. Then, more keenly, I realise I have never actually seen a vibrator in real life. This thought strikes me cold. I am going to seem like such a novice to Ellen if she wants me to explicitly describe something.

In a new browsing window, I search for sex toy shops nearby. I am certain I have seen some in town, there's at least one garish one on the high-street. This seems like an unusual way to spend a day off work, but I am nervously excited by the idea of buying myself a toy.

Before I change my mind, I head into town. The high street is quiet as most people are safely confined to their place of work, and the students have dispersed for summer term. I beeline to the nearest shop I had seen online but feel suddenly skittish as I near the entrance and end up speeding straight past. Perhaps the second, which is more of a lingerie shop, would be a bit more accessible. I try to make myself feel more confident as I walk there, standing straighter and smiling. This seems to help, and I sail through open doors of the shop. Annoyingly, I am immediately interrupted by a sales assistant who pops up to ask if I need any help. Shaking my head and trying to look less startled, I move quickly past the racks of underwear to the back of the shop where the sex toys are displayed. The lighting shifts to a pinkish hue.

I try to look as though I know what I am here for, hoping no-one else approaches me, but there are so many stacks of colourful boxes to choose from. Everything seems to be designed and packaged to be flashy and toy like. There is nothing discrete or sensual looking. In fact, none of the implements look sexually appealing to me; glitter embedded in solid, bobbled heads and long penis replications with extra digits. I pick up a couple of boxes at random to read the back, buying myself more time. Then another sales assistant approaches, arbitrarily shuffling boxes on her way, to ask how I am getting on. I cringe at the packages I am holding, tell her I am fine and smile until she drifts away. The pressure starts to mount. I blindly replace the items and make a swift move for the exit, avoiding looking at the sales assistants dotted around the escape route.

Propelled by nervous energy, I quickly walk back to the first shop, nestled away off the main high street. This time I boldly push the door open and try to relax. No one greets me at arrival; a lady at the cash desk glances up to see who has entered, then straight back down to her book. I feel relieved and scan the empty shop to orientate myself. It is a lot less commercial looking, no banners advertising sales and discounts, or flashy branded packaging; simply a shop which sold sex toys. A shop for adults that does not try to appeal to the inner child with sparkly marketing.

I catch sight of a display of vibrators and dildos in the corner, so I make my way over there. Next to the shelves of plain packaging, there is a display of unboxed toys, presumably so you could feel the textures before you committed to putting them in your vagina. I peruse the different sizes and shapes, not entirely convinced that I *do* want to put any of them inside my vagina. Then I see a white one which reminds me of the one in the video. It looks more like a nice piece of tech than a comedy penis: like a clean, sleek robotic mushroom. I pick up the box to read the description: "A powerful, battery powered vibrator for external stimulation." This is what I want.

Decisively I take the box to the counter and the middle-aged cashier smiles at me.

"A very popular model," she says, scanning the box and placing it in a white paper bag with handles. She also scans a pack of wet wipes, "These come free with your purchase," and packs them into the bag. She is so relaxed and business-like that my nerves stop jangling. I exit the shop very self-satisfied, then glance down at the bag and see that, though plain, the box still very obviously contains a vibrator. I curse myself for not bringing my backpack and practically jog home for fear of bumping into anyone I know.

My heart rate is through the roof when I get home. Feeling relieved that I evaded any close encounters and excited to try out my new toy, I sit cross-legged on the bed and open up the box. The vibrator is weighty in my hands as I flip open the battery slots and add some power. The front of the toy had a dial ranging from zero to ten. I twist the knob to one and the head begins to quietly buzz, I touch it to my arm and it tickles. I turn it up to three and the feeling intensifies, but my arm gets used to it quickly. Moving to my bra, a light tingle reverberates through to my nipple. I continue my exploration, realising I have some pent-up energy to burn.

19

No longer reliant on the maps app to direct me to Ellen's place, I am more aware of the buildings en route and notice a new cafe that has opened around the corner from my flat. An idea pops into my head; arriving at Ellen's with coffee and muffins might make the situation feel more relaxed and could win me some 'useful co-worker' brownie points. I join the queue inside and browse the selection before realising that I don't know how Ellen takes her coffee, or even if she drinks it. The barista leans over to take my order and I ask for two Americanos; Ellen can always add milk at her place.

I arrive at the house just after 3:30pm. As I knock on the door, Ted starts barking from the hallway and anxiety rises in my chest as all of the memories from last time rush back. When the door opens, I reflexively present the coffee. Ellen looks surprised, then pleased.

"Oh, thank God I haven't had time for a coffee today," she laughs and leads me through to the living room, Ted hot at my heels, curious about the muffin bag.

"Go to bed," Ellen says, pointing to a dog bed in the corner of the living room. Ted slumps over to his bed and flops down. I glance around at the room; papers strewn all over the floor, two laptops set up on the coffee table and a couple of plates with the remnants of past meals stacked behind them.

"Please excuse the mess, I'm swamped with new scenarios of moment. I would actually really appreciate your help."

I beam inwardly but try to seem chilled as I place the coffee on the table and gravitate to my familiar spot on the sofa. Ellen starts shuffling papers together then seems to change her mind.

"Do you mind if we finish up a couple of other projects before we get going on yours?" she asks.

"Not at all," I tell her, secretly pleased that I get to pry on other people's ideas.

"Excellent," she sounds tired. "Which coffee is mine?" she prises open the bag. "And muffins! Good thinking, this will keep us going."

"I got us both Americanos," I glance over, "the lowest risk coffee choice."

"Perfect," Ellen raises an eyebrow. "I only drink black coffee."

I am feeling very smug about my decision to stop at the coffee shop and Ellen appears to be indulging me. She plucks a muffin from the bag then takes a seat on the floor in front of one of the laptops. Taking a large bite from her muffin, she pats the floor next to her encouraging me to join her. I imitate her in sitting cross-legged on the carpet with a coffee.

"I hope you don't mind sitting on the floor," she says, "I've got quite used to it now. Seems to be better for my back. And the obvious lack of space for a desk." She swirls her coffee around indicating the small room.

The carpet is comfortable to sit on, but I worry about dropping crumbs everywhere. I see Ted eyeing up my muffin as I nibble at the edges. Ellen is opening yet more terminals on the laptop screen closest to her. Too many windows for my liking, it feels claustrophobic as I can't understand which are active. Ellen clocks my confused face.

"Right let me explain what is happening. I'm currently working on karate simulation."

I feel suddenly cold. I had assumed that people requested sexual or fantastical ideas, yet here is a perfectly mundane scenario. Now I feel weird about my request. Ellen seems to catch my thoughts and hurries to reassure me.

"This is actually more of a test simulation. It's at the request of Professor McAllister; he wants to see how accurately we can build very specific moves and respond in real-time to body movements. To enhance the responsiveness of our designs," she looks over to check I am following. "Normally client requests take priority over internal training designs, but I have been putting this off for a while, and Eric is due back this evening. No doubt he'll have edits anyway, but I wanted to have a draft prepared."

Ellen is done with her muffin so both hands are now free to type.

"If we open this window, you can see what I have built so far." She clicks open some blank windows on the screen closest to me, then navigates some code on her own screen. Two figures appear in the blank window. One is a middle-aged man in karate uniform, the other is almost a mirror image him but made out of tiny grids of green light.

"The guy dressed in karate gear is the subject in the scenario. The other figure represents the client. "Ellen side glances me to check I understand, I nod, wide-eyed. "Activity in this region provides the input for the scenario and the VR guy generates the appropriate output. In other words, what the client does influences how a scenario responds-" again she looks to me and stresses *"Within reason.* We build a range of *if functions* and appropriate behavioural responses. If the client acts out of bounds, sometimes I can amend the code from the control room, but we haven't developed responses for everything yet."

I'm in awe; I can barely use computational software to crunch data from my own research, let alone manipulate artificial intelligence.

"I have already scanned in and edited all of the moves the professor requested, I just need to build environment and check it for errors." I'm wondering how I can possibly help with this, but she seems to be enjoying explaining how it works, so I let her continue without question. "To be honest I usually just reuse backdrops because people barely notice their environments, but I don't have anything quite right for this. I was thinking about editing the theatre stage we used for you actually." She smiles at me, and I realise I am nodding a continuous slow movement, urging her to continue.

"Here, I'll show you," Ellen copies some code from one terminal to another and refreshes the video. Now the figures are stood atop the stage I had seen in my last scenario. "See it doesn't look quite right." She taps her fingers on the table, staying warmed up for when an idea comes. Then she turns to face me, "I'm thinking you could help with the environment build; would you mind looking up some images of karate halls for me to compare to please?"

"Yeah sure." I'm pleased to have a task to work on and quickly pull out my phone. Most of the images I find seem to have the same sorts of features, so after a few minutes I lean in to show her my phone screen. She exits what she had been typing in and streams my descriptions straight into her other code terminal. "It actually just looks like you need some rubber matting underfloor, wall-to-wall mirrors, and lots of space."

"Hmm," Ellen mumbles, "mirrors can be quite challenging in VR, I think I'll leave them out. So basically, I need to lay down a matted floor - perfect!" She sits quietly for a few moments typing, I steal a glance at her face in rapt concentration. She seems to have lost awareness of my presence, her mouth forming silent words as she tests out ideas. Then she smiles and nods, refreshes the video and shows a bright red matted floor. "That'll do for now, I think. Just need to run some trial-and-error scenarios." I start worrying that I'm not going to be any help at all when she says:

"While I do this, I was hoping you might be able to help me work on drafts for recent scenario requests? Some of these clients I have been dealing with for a while, and there's only so much rehashing of old scenarios you can do!" she laughs dryly. "It's good to have fresh ideas."

Now this is a task I can get excited for. The opportunity to delve into other people's fantasies and add my own touches. It makes me tingle thinking that a stranger will experience something I write.

Ellen seems to read my excitement and smiles, "I've already downloaded the drafts into a file, so they're anonymised, but some of them need more storyline or embellishments. I wondered whether you might be able to cast a fresh eye over them" Confident that she's hooked me in, she stops phrasing the request as a question.

Ellen unfolds her legs and stands; Ted stretches too and slinks over to her side.

"Let me grab my other laptop so you can get comfortable on the couch," she leaves the room, and Ted shadows her. I now feel compelled to stand and stretch out my limbs too. My knees click audibly so I am glad I waited until Ellen had left. I take a sip of my coffee, but it has gone cold. Probably just as well, I'm not sure the caffeine and excitement are a good combination.

When Ellen returns with the laptop clutched to her chest, I note that she has removed her jumper, which has mussed up her hair a little. I find this oddly endearing.

"OK, there's one client who is due in tomorrow evening, I'm a bit behind on their story so perhaps you could look at that first if you don't mind?" I assure her that I do not mind. I am actually itching to crack on.

She sits close to me on the sofa whilst the laptop loads, I watch her hands move gracefully across the keyboard typing in layers of passwords to get to the files. Her arm brushes mine and I feel its soft warmth. I wonder whether she notices small touches like I do. The laptop is slid over to my knee, a word heavy document is now open on the backlit screen.

She rises to get back to her work, "Do you want another drink?" she asks glancing at the unfinished coffee.

"No, I'm OK thanks," I smile, and return my eyes to the screen, watching her reposition by the coffee table in my unfocused gaze. There's a one-page document, heavily laden with details, I skim through. A three way with two women; the women are very specific in their appearance. Large breasts, large behinds, big lips. Voluptuous in excess. Half way down the page the descriptions change to actions; the client approaches and joins in with caressing the women (there is a side note that both women must feel extremely soft) and in return they touch the client's breasts.

"Wait, this is a woman?" I exclaim without thinking, realising I am interrupting Ellen who is looking intently at her screen. She turns to me, one eyebrow slightly cocked.

"Yes, why do you ask."

"Well, I was assuming it was a man based on the circumstances," I tell her, "But I guess that's just my own stereotypes coming into play."

Ellen snorts lightly. "Typical psychologist, trying to assume everyone's gender identity," she teases, "you'd be surprised who asks for what; stereotypes have no say in the Vie Lab." She starts typing on her laptop again, then pauses. "Having said that, this scenario is a bit bland so if you can think of some way to spice it up? This is her first request for women partners, so I don't want to push it too far, but you might be able help with that." She gives me a coy look that lingers with me even after she turns back at her screen.

I don't know whether to be flattered or offended by this. Does she mean assess how far I would take it as a novice, or how different my ideas could be. Before I can get back into reading, Ellen's house phone rings in the hallway and she unfolds herself to answer it. Ted plods after her.

I only hear half of the conversation, but Ellen sounds professional, so I assume it is work-related. When the call ends, she springs back into the room.

"Guess who doesn't have to work tonight," she sings, the jauntiness catching me off guard. I'm so used to her low, slow explanatory tone. Ted woofs.

"That was Eric," she re-enters the living room. "He's caught up at a conference in Liverpool, so he won't be back in time for tonight. That means I'll have a couple of days to finish this off." Ellen looks at her watch and then grins at me "Is it too early for wine?" It comes across as a rhetorical question. "Then we can get onto your scenario."

20

Ellen returns from the kitchen with two flutes of sparkling wine. It's the kind of alcohol that goes straight to my head and makes me giggle with little prompting. But it might be a good tonic for embellishing the manuscript I'm working on. She hands a glass to me and clinks with hers, then takes a long sip looking me directly in the eye. My cheeks are hot already.

"Are you alright finishing that three-way whilst I crack on with your scenario?" She asks, settling herself back down in front of the coffee table laptop.

"Yeah, that's cool," I say, cringing that Ellen is about to write something sexual for me, whilst I am right here. I remind myself that she does this every day, and that by now she's probably seen everything. Yet the flush in my cheeks trickles down my neck.

We return to a professional silence, both of us thinking hard and typing occasionally. Once I let my mind relax and put myself in the situation, I am able to expand the scenario. After a few rounds of writing and editing, I feel it's getting a bit cliché, so I read it out to Ellen.

"Nah, that's spot on. Exactly the sort of thing I reckon she would like," Ellen assures me. "It's a little bit different, but not *too* out there. She's a conservative woman, but the Vie Lab is her place to let go."

I nod, though Ellen hasn't looked away from her screen. I realise that writing has made me feel slightly aroused; for a moment I am tempted to ask Ellen that happens to her, but I feel that oversteps a boundary. She appears to be concentrating deeply, slightly hunched over the screen trying to get closer to what she is creating. Anticipation swells watching her hard at work writing something for me. I notice her wine glass is empty.

"Shall I top us up?" I ask.

She briefly looks away from the screen to say, "Oh yes please, the kitchen is just to the right from the hallway."

I gather our glasses and head in the direction she indicated. Ted follows me from the hallway to the kitchen.

"I haven't got any food, sorry." I tell him, opening the fridge. I see that Ellen also doesn't have any food. The kitchen is small, immaculate and clutter free. I get the impression she doesn't spend much time in here. I pull an opened bottle from inside the fridge door and pour the remainder of the bottle into our glasses. Ted pads behind me as I carry them back down the hallway, but crawls into a bed under the stairs as I re-enter the living room. I place Ellen's glass next to her on the table.

"Thanks," she says absentmindedly taking a gulp. I am about to sit back on the sofa when she says, "Hang on, can you come here a minute?"

I oblige and kneel down next to her on the floor. "You seem to be very specific about the type of vibrator you want," I nearly snort in my wine at how blunt she is, "but I don't think I've ever heard of it before. Is it real or do you want me to try and mock one up?"

"Oh, it is real, I actually went out and bought one," I tell her, trying to be as nonchalant as she is. I hold my wine glass up around my neck to try and hide the recurrent redness.

"What shop is it from?" she asks, opening an internet browser window "I'd like to see it."

"Sure," I stutter a little; she turns to me, expectant, and I catch a glint in her eye. Suddenly overcome with tipsy confidence, I lean over her to type the name of the vibrator. Images cascade down the screen instantaneously. I click one that shows it *in situ.*

"Jeez that's massive!" she exclaims, "That can't all go in surely?"

I laugh, a nervous jangle. "No, it's erm, external stimulation only." I'm tripping over the words, but she doesn't seem to notice, her face leaning closer to the screen.

"Oh, I see," she draws the words out then pauses. "I think I have something *similar."*

Before I can acknowledge this fact, she's on her feet and out the door. I hear her tell Ted to "staaay," as she passes him in the hallway.

I become aware of the hammering of my pulse as await her to return; I've never chatted to anyone about sex toys before so I'm not sure what the boundaries are. Ellen returns with her arms full; she places another bottle of wine on the table.

Sitting down next to me on the sofa, she reveals three plastic toys and two small remote controls.

"So, this is very clever," she launches straight in, handing me a large velvety bean, about six by two inches in my hand, and a plastic remote control. "You turn it on using the little switch there," she points to one of the buttons on the remote "and change the intensity with the slider," she pushes my finger up the small, notched scale.

I press the on switch, but nothing happens to the bean. Ellen laughs, "Ohh you've got mine," she says, "I'll do yours."

Suddenly the bean in my hand jumps to life, pulsating rhythmically. "You can turn up the intensity," she says, and the pulsating quickens. She leans in closer to me and takes the bean from my hand, holding it to the crook of my arm where it tickles. I giggle, and her smile broadens pulling tiny dimples into her cheeks. The wine is making me feel playful and her sitting so close is intoxicating; I chance touching the bean in my hand to her leg.

"Hey, I'm ticklish," she laughs and bats me away, then reaches for the other toy, longer with controls on the chassis.

"I think this one is a similar model to what you have. But it probably feels quite different to the others," she turns it on and runs the tip down the inside of my arm. This one has a much more penetrating vibration.

"Admittedly, slightly more *electric toothbrush*," Ellen says and the corners of her eyes crinkle. "Which do you prefer?"

"This one, the first one," I say nodding to my right arm where she still presses the bean, my voice cracks a little. Ellen switches the larger off and lays it back on the table.

"Okay, should we use these little ones in your scenario then?" She looks me in the eye, a steady grey penetration, and I wonder if she is leaving it up to me to end the game. I nod "Sounds good," my voice slipping away. I want to seem more in control of myself, so I push the slider up, increasing the pulsations so they are audible. Ellen seems pleased by this move, which emboldens me, and I take hold of her hand, guiding the toy down to where I want it.

Suddenly she is close, her eyes alight, her fingers drawing soft pulsating circles. I grasp hold of her arm triggering an explosive orgasm.

Reflexively, I let go, and she relaxes her hand. She turns the toy off, and the room falls silent.

"Well, I'm glad we clarified that," she says, brightly sliding back to her seat on the floor.

I remain sat, my legs like jelly. Ellen starts to type again, glancing at the toys presumably for reference. I feel bewildered, having never gone from sexual encounter back to normality with no mutual resolution, or, at the very least, intimacy. The sexual atmosphere that seemed to build so quickly, dissolved instantly. An unpleasant thought creeps in; this is a strange, one-way lust.

"I think I'll head home." I say, surprising myself a little.

Ellen twists around, her face puzzled "Are you tired of creating scenarios?"

I shake my head.

"Well why not stay and help me then. Or at least finish your wine," she nods to the glass in my hand, dimples creeping back. Her stomach growls into the silence.

"I am suddenly ravenous; do you want to order some food?" She asks, pulling up a list of takeaways on her laptop without awaiting my response.

My brain is addled with post-coital confusion. Are we on a date now? Or are we working late? Is she trying to politely ignore me coming in her living room? Or was that part of her plan? Before I properly consider my actions, I realise that I am standing.

"Sorry, I have just remembered I need to get back," I say feebly.

She furrows her brow and gestures at her screen. "But what about food?"

"I'll just grab something on the way home," I say. The more I talk, the more committed I am to leaving. I back quickly into the hall quickly causing Ted to let out an unsettled grumble from under the stairs.

"Alright, well if you have to get back." Ellen follows, trailing off into the awkward silence I have made. "Let me know if you want to pop in another day this week, I've got plenty of stuff to be working on if you want to help."

I nod and step out into the warm summer evening to breathe. The intoxications have rushed in all together and my legs feel unsteady, my thoughts hazy.

As I turn to say a final goodbye, Ellen leans in and kisses me fully on the lips.

21

After kissing me, Ellen practically closes the door in my face. I stand for a minute contemplating knocking again but my brain is whirring. The wine, lack of food, mixed signals. My face burns as I hurry back into town.

On the way I stop at the nearby local supermarket and slowly pace the aisles trying to choose easy food for dinner. The bright lights and sharp changes in temperature are jarring in my heightened state of awareness, but I feel a weird sense of comfort being in a shop I regularly peruse. Faking normality whilst I get my head together. I pick up a ready-made pasta dinner to put in the oven and grab a bag of salad. There is an offer to make it dinner for two with a bottle of wine, but I decline the offer. More wine might not end well tonight, I need to get my head straight.

As soon as I get home, I text Riya. The situation feels too bizarre for me to process alone I need an outsider opinion. I decide it is a bit out of the blue to explain that Ellen had kissed me given that I hadn't warmed Riya up with the preamble. So,

I ask if I can meet her for lunch at work tomorrow. I must sound worried because she doesn't even take the piss out of me for coming onto campus on my day off.

I abandon my shopping in the kitchen and flop onto the bed fully clothed. Wine in my blood amplifies my emotions and I don't know whether to cry or laugh about what happened at Ellen's. You can't just carry on working after making someone orgasm, can you? Then kiss them at the front door as they leave. That is the very essence of blowing hot and cold. I glance at my phone to see if she had, by chance, decided to text me. She had not.

◆ ◆ ◆

When I wake on Thursday morning, there is a text from Ellen. My heart jolts seeing her name and all of the memories from last night hurtle back at one. The message simply reads "I finished your scenario," with a smiling face, sent at 3am. Wow, she is a workaholic. I start to plan a reply, then recall how we parted ways last night. She could have acknowledged that situation. A swell of annoyance rises in my stomach, and I decided not to reply for a while. I will eat some breakfast and relax a little first.

Shuffling groggily into the kitchen, I browse the cupboards for suitable breakfast food but find nothing edible. Plenty of herbs, spices and condiments, but nothing with any nutritional value. The pasta dinner lies warm and sad on the kitchen counter. A depressing waste. It is probably time I sort my life out and go to the *proper* supermarket instead of getting by on bits and pieces.

123

I dress quickly and find my bike helmet in the cupboard by the front door. It's been a while since I've done a *big shop*, so I anticipate filling both bike panniers. Light streaming into my flat assures me that it is a beautiful day; a bike ride will do me and my dark mood some good. To cheer myself up slightly, I decide to cycle to the fancier supermarket on the other end of town.

My bike leans limply against the rack at the back of my flats. I almost wish one of my neighbours would pop out in time for me to joke about the bike being two-tired to stand up. Instead, I sigh at the bad joke to myself and unravel the slightly rusty lock. As it is after peak traffic time the roads are likely to be fairly quiet, but I decide to take a slight detour to avoid any chance of seeing Ellen near Ryan's bookbinding. The gentle, warm wind on my face feels good. This is exactly what I needed: to focus my energies on navigating the road by bike and stop obsessing over the Vie Lab situation.

The cycle takes less than twenty minutes, and by the time I arrive at the whole food supermarket I have perked up considerably. I lock up my bike and pick up a shopping basket before entering the shop. I had forgotten how much I like this place. The fruit and vegetables are laid out in a colourful array, being spritzed by mists of water for no apparent reason. A lady in an apron offers me a sample of cheese with a recommended wine accompaniment. Staff stand behind displays of meat and fish, acting like local butchers and fishmongers. Customers come here to browse and chat.

After picking out some fruit and vegetables, I head to the fresh bread section and choose a selection of mix and match rolls. Down the next aisle, I pick up a new type of cereal with a multitude of vitamins added. I decide to treat myself to an overpriced carton of smoothie, then browse some of the more expensive wines. As I flick open the lid of a shampoo container to query the fragrance, I notice my phone vibrating in my pocket. I lower my heavy basket to the floor and glance at the screen. It is Ellen. I decide to ignore it. I couldn't think of any conversation we might have that would be appropriate for the health and beauty aisle of a supermarket. My head feels fuzzy as I watch her name flash for what feels like minutes. Then the screen goes black again. I quickly cast around to see if anyone had seen me stare, horrified, at my phone, but luckily the aisle is quiet.

My mood flips back to unsettled and am keen to retreat home. The checkout area is empty, and I walk straight up to the sole cashier perched behind a till. He is bright and cheery, chipping away at the dark mood that had descended. It feels impossible to fester in my sulk. The shopping *just* fits in the pannier bags; a satisfying feeling. My ride home takes a little longer with the added weight.

I get back and feel the rushing security of my flat as I close the door behind me. Realising how hungry I am, I warm one of my bakery items and pour a glass of juice. Sitting by the window overlooking the city I try to un-tense my muscles. A few days off is exactly what I need. I realise that I have been applying the same obsessive energies at the Vie Lab project as I had placed on my own PhD. Thinking about it constantly and wondering whether there was anything I could be doing. A one-way ticket to burnout town.

My ringtone pulls me out of the focused relaxation. Ellen's name on the screen again. May as well get it over with:

"Hello," I say, in my best attempt at a neutral tone.

"Oh, thank god, I was worried about you!" Ellen answers with strain in her voice "I got pretty absorbed in working on your project after you left, but I realised you hadn't text to say you got home OK, then I got worried." She falls silent leaving me space to jump in with my reasoning. I can't think of anything quick enough, so she continues. "I was so inspired to finish that scenario I stayed up half the night!"

I know I'm supposed to mirror her enthusiasm, but I've tangled everything up with my feelings for her and that feels vulnerable. I want to appear measured and unemotional.

"I can't wait to see it," I say; the words are true I just can't express it in my voice.

"Do you want to come over this afternoon and try it out?" she presses on keenly. I pause. Part of me wants to, but I feel it might be better, *healthier,* to have a break from the intensity. At least briefly.

"Sorry I have plans today," I say too quickly. She makes a dejected sound and I feel bad that she stayed up all night to finish it. "How about tomorrow?" I offer.

"Actually, that probably makes more sense," she says perking up. "I have a client in at seven, and I should probably have a nap before, so yes tomorrow. How about 4pm? We could sneak some dinner in afterwards, before my evening client arrives," she sounds so delighted that I agree. We hang up.

Excitement starts to creep back in. The idea of experiencing my scenario elaborated by Ellen is one thing, but dinner afterwards sounds like a date. Don't overthink it, I tell myself, just see what happens.

22

Riya and I decide to meet somewhere different than our usual coffee shop haunt. There is a small Indonesian restaurant that has a good lunch menu just off campus, it seems quiet enough that we could discuss my situation without too much concern.

Riya greets me with a hug. "Have you lost weight? Feeling a little bony around your shoulders there!" she prods my collar bone. I reassure her that I had a substantial breakfast, but mentally reflect I could have lost a little from the meals I have inadvertently missed lately. To overcompensate, prove a point to Riya and myself, I order a large curry. Not the sort of thing I'd normally choose for lunch, but the indulgence is exactly how a day off from work should feel. Riya orders a lighter stir fry, claiming that she has a project meeting mid-afternoon and doesn't want to fall asleep.

Riya doesn't bother with the pleasantries, and as soon as we have ordered she delves straight in. "So, what's going on? I've never seen you like this before; you've gone all pale. Tell me."

Where to start.

"I've been getting more involved in the Vie Lab research," I start.

Riya nods and says, "I thought you might have," to which I give a puzzled look. "It's exactly your sort of thing," she explains. "Cognitive manipulation, that's why I invited you along in the first place."

She's right, but on reflection I wouldn't have attended so readily if she had been upfront about her sexual fantasy aspect. It's hard to know if she realises this, or whether it didn't cross her mind. A question for another time.

I continue, "Well anyway, I went to a couple more sessions, then started helping Ellen on the development side."

"Oh, that's interesting," Riya interrupts. "I always wondered how they made it virtual reality, but I sort of felt like knowing would ruin the illusion."

"Not really," I say, "it's quite complex what goes on, I don't think I've scratched the surface in my understanding." I take a sip of water, "What I find most intriguing is how Ellen writes nearly all of the scenarios."

"Hmm, I don't think that's true," Riya interjects. "I wrote my own story, right down to the shape of the doctor's dick," she whispers the last section across the table, her face twisting into a mischievous grin.

"Well, yes, I imagine a few people do write their own ideas. But Ellen makes it feel real. Not just the build of the people and the environment looking a certain way, but the way they it *feels* like it's actually happening."

"I think that's probably down to the way the programme is set up-" Riya says, pausing to receive her meal. I take mine and our table water is refilled, then she continues "The whole point of it is to mess with your mind, tap into your thought processes in a computer-generated environment."

I think about this for a second, it's a good point. "But Ellen -"

"OK I see what's going on," Riya says through a mouthful of noodle. "You don't want to talk about the *Lab*, you want to talk about *Ellen,* don't you?"

Bloody hyper-perceptive psychologist friends. The blush creeps up my chest to my face and ears.

"Ha got it!" she exclaims. "Now tell me what's bothering you really."

"I have a crush on Ellen," I admit.

Riya lays down her fork and listens more carefully.

"It started off as a general intrigue in her as a researcher, but I've developed more of an attraction to her the more time I've spent with her."

"I didn't know you were into women?" Riya says, one eyebrow half lifted.

I laugh a little, "I don't know, maybe I'm not, it could just be Ellen."

"So, has anything happened? Anything interesting I mean?"

"A few bits," I can't decide which things I feel comfortable saying.

Riya makes a girly noise reserved for occasions such as this.

"But not necessarily in the right order," I try to make light of how I see the situation in my mind. Riya looks confused,

"What is the right order?" she asks.

I lean in and we both hold our cutlery still. "Well firstly she made me come using one of her sex toys, and later she kissed me." I practically mouth the words, Riya strains to hear

129

correctly. "But straight after the kiss, she closed the door in my face."

"Whaat!" Riya can't hide a laugh she tries to suppress "You're right, the order seems off. But perhaps it makes sense with elaboration?"

"So, I was at her house last night, helping out with some scenarios. We had some wine, I hadn't eaten any dinner, so I got a bit tipsy, and she was showing me some of her inspiration. One thing just led to another-"

"Oh my god did you have sex with her?" Riya exclaims.

"That was literally everything that happened, just some one-sided orgasming." I mouth the word orgasming, just in case anyone is listening. "It didn't go any further. Except straight back to work." Riya pulls a face. "I know, it was a bit awkward. I thought it was best if I left, but then she kissed me."

"I always thought she was a bit weird," Riya says, picking up her fork again.

"What do you mean?" A defensive edge to my question.

"I dunno, she was always a bit cold and impersonal with me. Very *peculiar*."

"You've only met her a few times."

"Well, you can get a feel for these things pretty quickly. I don't think she knows how to interact with people in the real world."

"I disagree, I think she is very perceptive and creative." I realise my voice is raised, and the waiters are looking over so lower it. "You'd have to be to design such intricate representations of humans."

"Sorry, I didn't mean to be rude," Riya says a little sheepishly. "Perhaps she's just not that practiced at out of work social interaction."

The comment hangs awkwardly and I can't think of a good reply. I don't want Riya to comment on the situation any more so quickly change the subject to something I know she'll want to discuss.

"Anyway, how is it going with Sal," I ask, referring to the guy she recently started dating. Riya's face lights up again.

"Great actually, thanks. He stayed over again last night. And he likes that law drama I'm always telling you about *Truth For Glory* - did you ever watch it?" I shake my head "I like that he and I have similar tastes," she smiles. "And the fact her knows his way around a woman's body doesn't hurt," she snorts.

"So, I take it you won't be booking out any more time in the Lab?" I ask her.

"'Hmm not right now," she says scooping up her last pieces of noodles. "I'm pretty busy at the moment so I'd rather spend free time with people. But I'm not ruling it out in future, it's a cool idea for sure."

I want to tell her about my Vie Lab idea for tomorrow, but I feel like it's verging on obsessive to turn another conversation back that way, so I ask some more probing questions about her new relationship whilst we finish off our food.

"Why don't you give the dating app a try," Riya pushes as we collect the bill. "It could be good to have some different dating options if Ellen is giving you mixed signals." I nod noncommittally. "You could see if there are any women who take your fancy," she adds, as if this may be a game-changer. I know that she doesn't understand my feelings, but neither do

131

I. Perhaps she is right that I need to broaden my dating experiences. People always tell me that's what your twenties are for.

23

Taking Riya's advice that evening, I download one of the more popular dating apps. Even the landing page makes me cringe; fireworks flashing behind the registration screen and tiny love hearts dotting the i's in the form. I enter my details and continue to the interests page. I decide not to add that my personal hobbies include reading psychology papers and obsessively researching virtual reality software. Instead, I say I am in to theatre, art, reading and drinking; all four do seem to be on the increase lately.

A loading page begins to count up how many matches I have so I go to the kitchen, crack open a bottle of wine and pour myself a generous glassful. When I return to my phone I have 112 *best picks* from the local area, lined up for my perusal. It feels like a chore to browse this many profiles, so I shamelessly go through each display photo searching for any twinge of attraction.

I can't decide if I'm not in the mood to do this now, or whether being hung up on Ellen is putting me off. I decide to persevere at least the end of the glass. A couple of pages later, I come across an intriguing face. "Seth, 29," it says above the photo of a handsome man with blonde, wavy hair. It says he is online, so when I start browsing his photos, I am encouraged to chat with him. I ignore this for the time being, though I am mildly interested in talking to him. We appear to have been matched because he is a scientist too, but we don't seem to share any hobbies in common. He is more into motocross racing, skiing and cave exploration; all things I cannot understand the pleasure in. But he is quite cute, smiling a large, white-toothed grin in all his photos.

I finish the glass of wine and decide to send him a message, contemplating what you are supposed to say to online strangers when you only know a handful of generic facts. Sighing, I reside to asking a question about his research. At the very least it's a good way to rule him out if the answer is either boring or non-existent. The app informs me that Seth will be saved to my *quick picks* zone for future reference. I wait a couple of minutes for a reply, but none comes, so I pour myself another glass of wine and continue browsing. Does everyone find this tedious, I wonder?

By page eight I have lost interest in browsing, and Seth is no longer online so I quit the app feeling a mixture of disappointment and relief.

The evenings feel longer without the countdown to work the next day. I decide to indulge in some self-care - a routine Riya seems to live by - and apply a hair mask before bed. I circle the flat turning off lights and checking doors and windows are locked, then stand for a moment looking out at the quiet space between the flats. I wonder how many other people are taking themselves to bed at this moment.

I climb into my cold, crisp sheets and turn my phone to night mode. Just before it activates, a message notification flashes on the homepage. It is from Ellen:

"Looking forward to tomorrow night x"

A kiss! The first kiss she's ever sent, digitally. This minor character addition officially indicating the relationship moving out of the professional zone. In the quiet darkness of my bedroom, I let out a tiny noise of excitement.

"Me too. Night x" I reply and promptly turn off the lamp, so I can sleep on the high.

24

The wealth of free time allows me to catch up on my neglected correspondence. I break the morning in with a black coffee and a couple hours of digital browsing. Sitting with my phone and laptop by the window, I run through the unopened emails, texts, threads, group chats, images, videos and snippets; congratulating friends on recent engagements, pregnancies and promotions; commenting on holiday photos, graduations and well-presented meals; realising how out of touch I am with many of the friends who didn't live in Manchester.

When my eyelids start to click dryly, I realise that I need to change my focus. I prepare myself a mezze of food with things in the fridge and stand in the kitchen picking at it. I cast my vision around the flat to relax my eyes and notice the canvas of the Virginia Howl woman I had abandoned earlier in the week. The resemblance to Ellen is a little unsettling, even though I am sure only I would notice it; the skill is certainly not portrait standard. Still, I feel a compulsion to have another crack. I finish off the lunch and plug my phone into the music system, taking time to pick out the right album. Tegan and Sara's *The Con* takes me back to college, hunching over a lightbox redrawing the expressive edges of an Egon Schiele figure, wired in to my portable CD player.

I collect and soak the brushes I had left to crust over at the end of my last session, ashamed of the neglect of my brand-new set. I set out my paints again and flick through the Virginia Howl book, looking for another inspiration. The same fair skinned model I had been drawn to last time crops up a few times. One pose is particularly compelling; she lies in bed, duvet crumpled, head resting on her hand, her gaze turned away, disinterested. I sketch, and by the end of the album have filled in most of the background colours. The music app skips on to *So Jealous* and I sit painting for another 45 minutes. The background and textures and looking a bit flat, but I am pleased with the progress I am making on the face.

The music fades out momentarily to allow a notification to jangle through on my phone. I glance up at the time and see that it has just gone two o'clock. Suddenly I feel grossly unprepared for the 4pm meeting. The brushes lie to ruin again as I dash to the shower.

◆ ◆ ◆

Duran Duran sidetracks my thoughts from the situation as I weave through town to Ryan's Bookbinding. I take a minute to regain some stillness as I stand outside the shop, preparing to press the buzzer. When I do, and I hear Ellen's voice running the drill about the shop being closed, my legs feel suddenly heavy. She lets me in, and I make a conscious effort to ascend every step without tripping, whilst mentally cycling through different greetings options.

I enter the reception area and see Ellen behind the desk, her hair pulled up to a bun and dressed in her business attire. She doesn't look right like this now that I've spent time with her casually. I feel instant dread that she will treat me like a client, and I won't be able to respond appropriately.

Her neutral expression melts into a soft smile. Perhaps it is obvious that I am nervous because she comes around the desk and takes hold of my hand. Hers is small and soft in mine, but she clasps firmly and leads me through to the control room. A room I definitely didn't need leading to after three sessions here, but I appreciate the touch of her hand, it feels like a warm up to the session. Though it is already feeling like too much stimulation.

When she twists to face me in the room, I am almost certain that she is going to kiss me, but she just drops my hand, smiles and turns to face the consoles. "Are you ready to go?" she asks, her back to me.

"Oh yeah, sure," the first word I have uttered since arriving. I take myself through to the Vie Lab.

25

Ellen assures me that she can see and hear me from the other room, that the exit code is still *end game.* The lights reset and then the room is light, but almost exactly the same. The only additions appear to be a door in the far corner, a small set of drawers on wheels and a long white bed. Attached to the bed are four shackles: two in the middle and two at the base. I can imagine how they will be used. I tense up waiting to see what comes through the door.

Moments later, the doorknob turns, and three tall men enter; the first is pale with greying hair and round spectacles, smartly dressed; the other two look curiously like the older man, though at least twenty years younger, though at least twenty years younger with darker hair and sharper eyes.

"Good afternoon, Nicole, I am Victor," the older man says in a low, refined voice, leaning in to shake my hand. "These are my assistants Alpha and Beta," the twins give a nod from their position flanking Victor. "Shall we begin?" Victor asks, not to me, but to his assistants who stride towards me, hook their arms through mine and lift me onto the bed. One proceeds to undress me, gently unbuttoning my dress and pulling it above my head, the other takes the dress, folds it, and places it to the side. Both then work together to remove my tights and knickers, laying them neatly on top of the dress. Finally, my bra is unhooked and tidied away.

The twins each take hold of an arm and lower me to a lying position. Their skin feels soft against mine. My wrists and ankles are placed in the shackles and the leather fastenings tightened. Victor is standing at the end of the bed, observing, nodding occasionally. I feel very exposed with my legs spread so widely in front of him, but he does not seem to have acknowledged this, his gaze flitting between the twins as they work. When I am securely fastened to the bed, the assistants step aside to receive further direction from Victor.

"Very good," he praises. "Now we need to prepare her for the devices." They nod and step back towards me in unison. Their hands begin to caress my breast and abdomen; warm and gentle. After a nod from Victor, the twin to my left begins stroking my inner thigh, sending a shudder through me. I am just starting to relax into it when I see that Victor is now taking something out of the drawers next to the bed. I recognise the long mushroom headed vibrator, and the short bean shaped one from Ellen's place. He holds one in each hand, and noting my gaze, says "I think it's time for the blindfold."

Alpha holds my head up slightly as Beta wraps a length of fabric around my head and ties it at the back. My head is laid back on the bed almost tenderly. With all sense of vision removed I feel very vulnerable, which makes the nerves in my body stand on end. No one is touching me now, and I feel like the minute they do, I'll jump out of my skin.

I hear the low vibration of the toys being switched on.

"Alpha, this one is for you, and Beta you take this one." Victor directs the twins. I wonder which toy they were each assigned then realise it doesn't make any difference.

"Remember to take it slowly, we don't want her to climax too quickly," his voice has a sharp, no-nonsense tone.

First, I recognize the pulsating bean as it is applied, I pull away with the shock of the contact, but relax as a gentle rhythm begins. I tense again as the cold head of the mushroom vibrator slides up the inside of my thigh. Being out of control is both invigorating and nerve-wracking. Every new touch sends a bolt of stimulation through my whole body. The vibrator reaches the top of my leg and continues up as the bean is removed. I clench automatically but this amplifies the sensation, which is already on the verge of being too intense. Almost as soon as I feel this, the toy begins to move back down my thigh.

The routine repeats itself in an orchestrated rhythm and I start to perspire as the intensity builds and is curtailed over and over. My hips rock in anticipation of the pleasure; trying to extend the building sensation, craving the relief.

"See how she desperately wants to climax," Victor says, speaking as though I am not there. "We mustn't let her."

There is a pause, a brief absence of touch, and my body throbs. Then the routine changes. The toys slide back, slick and slow. I try to tip over the edge, but they are removed before I can. I am writhing, half infuriated, half intoxicated. Then suddenly it all stops and falls quiet. A complete absence of touch and sound.

I open my eyes but there is still darkness. Then a crack of light as a door open and Ellen clicks over to me swiftly. I wonder if I have broken the programme somehow. She kneels and I start to ask what's happening, but she covers my mouth with her hand. Her other hand slides down between my still spread legs. I orgasm almost immediately, intensely, under her assertive touch.

"I wanted to be the one who made you come," she says when my body falls still. Then she stands back up and leaves the room again. I lie on my back, drained.

When the blood circulates back to my extremities, I dress and haul myself into the control room, Ellen has already shut down the computers and is hovering in the reception area.

"Dinner is on me!" she exclaims when I enter, evidently back in business mode, glazing over the fact that she just got hands on with my intimate scenario. A flurry of emotions starts to twist inside me; how can she switch this on and off. But then she is smiling, a full dimpled grin that cuts through my anguish and I follow her. I wonder whether I dreamt the end of the scenario. Fell asleep somehow. I examine her face as we come into the bright evening; she looks more animated than usual.

"That took longer than I expected," Ellen says as we pick up pace, "I didn't do a practice run through like I normally would with a new scenario."

"Why didn't you trial it?" I ask, glad I didn't know this ahead of time.

"I liked the idea that it was a scenario just for you, no-one else had experienced it." Ellen side glances at me and smiles "Besides, I didn't really have time."

We turn off the main high-street onto a smaller street with restaurants and bars. She leads me into a quiet bistro and asks for a table for two. It's early so the place is fairly empty. We are seated by the window.

"Sorry that this is so rushed," Ellen says quietly as she scans the menu. "I was looking forward to spending more time with you, but I've got that bloody client soon."

"No, it's fine, I've got stuff to do this evening anyway." Ellen looks up over the menu and I am tempted to spin a yarn about having a date to assess her response, but I decide not to risk it.

The waitress comes to take a drink order. "I'm not drinking alcohol," Ellen says. "But obviously you can." I decide against it, might as well stay as clearheaded as she is even if I don't have to go back to work. We both order sparkling water.

"I'm actually ready to order food if you are," Ellen says, catching the waitress as she turns on her heels. I haven't even read the menu.

"Sure, I'll have the salmon please," I pick randomly from the middle of the menu.

"And I'll have the mushroom pasta please," Ellen says, closing her menu and passing it back to the waitress.

Ellen waits until the waitress is at a safe distance away before leaning in and whispering, "So, did you enjoy your scenario?" she rests her chin on her hand, and I am reminded of the woman in the Howl painting.

I think for a moment, unsure what the truthful answer is. "I enjoyed the very end," I say, unable to stop the flicker of smile turning my mouth.

"Which bit? Oh, *that* bit. Yes, well that was unscripted," she laughs a little, and a tiny blush hits her cheeks. "But what about the characters, did you like them?"

"Honestly, I found them a bit creepy."

"Oh, how come?" Ellen seems a bit dejected by this response.

"OK, I get the voyeuristic older man orchestrating the pleasure, but what was up with the silent twins, they felt like weird androids?"

Ellen breaks out into peals of laughter. It's infectious, and I giggle even though I don't know why she's laughing.

"Oh god I can't believe you noticed that! You are right, they *are* duplicates of the same persona. I just shifted the age and a few other details. I meant to make the other two more dissimilar, but I ran out of time and –" She trails off.

"You thought I wouldn't notice."

"Well, yes. You *were* blindfolded for most of it. Besides, I mostly liked the juxtaposition of passive players and active players. Just made a change from the regular scenarios where everyone gets a hand in," she laughs at her own pun, and I force a smile. I can't help feeling a bit put out that she hadn't put the same effort into the scenario as she usually seemed to. The disappointment must be painted on my face because she shifts to take hold of my hand and my pulse leaps at the gesture. "I'm sorry if it wasn't what you hoped, I just got a bit overexcited. I've read so many blasé scripts, I was pleased when you seemed to be after something a little different. And I was excited to finish it."

The food arrives, and Ellen withdraws her hand. I am irked by the fleetingness of our intimacy.

"No, I did enjoy it," I insist, not wanting to let her down. "It just threw me off a little."

Ellen seems content with this and tucks into her pasta. I haven't really got the appetite for the salmon dish I've ordered, my stomach churns nervously.

"Have you tried any other weird ideas?" I ask, taking all of my self-restraint not to add 'with other people' to the end of the sentence.

Ellen covers her mouth as she swallows a mouthful of food, then says: "Maybe you'll just have to find out for yourself."

Excitement and fear strike me at once. I'm not sure about my boundaries yet, and Ellen seems to enjoy pushing the limits. I am intrigued to know what sorts of things she has written and experienced, but at the same time I'm worried that if I find it all out too soon it'll scare me.

Ellen finishes her pasta rapidly, I force down several mouthfuls of salmon, so I don't seem too fussy, and tuck my cutlery to one side when she does.

"Are you done already?" She asks me doubtfully.

Yeah, I'm still quite... satisfied from earlier," I say, patting my stomach in mock satiety. Ellen looks pleased, then flags down the waitress to get the bill.

"Again, sorry I have to get back. I'll make it up to you though."

"You better had!" I say in jest, but I hear the neediness in my tone.

"How about tomorrow?" She asks, pulling her purse from her bag. "I could make you dinner at my place?"

"Why don't you come to mine for a change, I feel like I'm always drinking your wine."

"OK fine, tomorrow night at your place," she smiles. "I'll bring dessert if you cook something delicious for us?"

I enjoy flirty Ellen, much better than professional Ellen. I agree to the terms of our date and the waitress arrives with the card machine to pay. "Are you paying separately?" she asks.

I reach to my bag, but Ellen stops me. "This is on me," she says.

Surely a date.

26

Ellen and I part ways outside of the restaurant with no physical acknowledgement, but I feel sure there is a new energy between us. I almost offer to walk her back to the lab, but decided against it, we had planned the next day after all. So, I casually walk in the opposite direction.

A little way down the street, I turn to see if Ellen is still in view and catch her about to turn a corner. She is walking in unison with a tall man, they are talking. My initial reaction is panic that the man is hassling her, but quickly see she shows no indication of distress. Ellen probably knows the guy. I calm myself and carry on walking. Emotions are definitely heightened this evening; a tiny hum of excitement still resonating from the date.

Back at my flat, the air seems stuffy and close. I roll open a couple of windows and sit on the chair to look out into the small space outside. An unusual quiet descends and I find my brain mellowing. Then I remember my phone has been silent and dormant in my bag all day. I pull it out and immediately the stillness is filled with noise. There are so many notifications I have missed. Replies from conversations I started earlier in the day, as well as a banner from the dating app, informing me that I have messages. I am mildly intrigued by the latter.

I log in to the app and see that I have a reply from Seth, the man I messaged last night, along with two further messages to be opened. I open the reply from Seth first.

"Hello Nicole, thanks for the message. I am a biologist at the Uni, I'm working on stem cells. How about you? I'm not a massive fan of this online messaging thing, would you like to meet up for a coffee some time? Seth,"

I feel a bit uneasy about the online dating situation now that Ellen and I have a date arranged. It feels disloyal. But maybe dispersing my interests would mean that not so much rests on every interaction with Ellen. Maybe it would add perspective. And I feel like it would please Riya if I actually went on a date as a result of her suggestion to try the app.

I type back "Oh cool, I work at the Uni too - Psychology. Yeah, we could meet at the Coffee Machine on Tuesday? Should still be empty with students' holidays – Nicole."

Seth's profile does not say he's online, so I don't expect a response any time soon. I check the other two messages. Both are generic "how are you?" questions. I don't bother replying.

It's just gone nine when I wake up on Friday. I scroll through the news on my phone as light shards through the blinds creep up my body. There's a notebook in my bedside cabinet that I used to scrawl notes for my thesis on if I couldn't sleep, I dig it out to plan a shopping list for tonight. I find a couple of Moroccan style dishes that can be prepared in advance. In the notebook, I jot down the ingredients, then a note to buy extra wine and candles.

The midweek shop is a revelation to me. My panniers let me down by not allowing me to squeeze all of the food into the two bags, so I have to balance one plastic carrier on the handlebars. I cycle home slowly, the extra weight biasing my steering. Half way back I become aware of a car driving uncomfortably close behind me. I tuck in closer to the pavement and slow down, so they can overtake, but they don't. The car continues to crawl behind me and my heart rate increases. I crane my head around and see an all-black car; the passenger side window is winding up. I can't see inside because of the tinted windows. My brain goes to the bad places I've seen on TV, and I mount the curb accidentally, rolling to a stop in shock. The car drives away.

I stand on the pavement, balancing my bike and breathing hard. In hindsight my reaction seems melodramatic; why be alarmed by a cautious driver? But I can't shake the unease I felt being followed like that. Apparently, my emotions are still on hyperdrive. I walk a little way with my bike in tow, then hop back on and pedal home spurred by adrenaline.

When I get back, I decide to try and finish off my painting, acutely aware that I might not make the time after my leisurely week off. I make a coffee and sit down in my painting zone on the floor of the living room. Lightly touching the canvas with my fingertips, I note with satisfaction that the initial layer from last night has dried. I browse for *Surfer Rosa* by Pixies and plug in. The powerful percussion of *Bone Machine* stirs up some inspiration and I decide on a finished image for the painting.

I spend the length of *Surfer Rosa*, *Doolittle* and *Bossanova* glued to the floor painting highlights and shadows on the face. It doesn't much look like the Howl model, but at least it resembles a face. As my phone transitions to *Trompe de Monde*, I finally acknowledge the pressing need to urinate. I nip to the toilet and back, and as I am about to sit down realise that I've probably finished my painting. It's definitely not fine art, but I feel it is a good effort, so I decide to let it be. I place the canvas in the corner to dry and set about collecting my brushes to wash. The packaging has the receipt stuck to it, so I detach and start to crumple up to bin when I see *timforart dot com* in slanted cursive. I had completely forgot about the guy in the art shop and his painting website. I crack open my laptop and wake it from sleep to find the website.

For some reason only wedding caricatures had stuck in my mind from the conversation, so I am surprised to be presented with a full portfolio of fine art paintings on the home page. Tim is evidently a very skilled artist. I click through to a page showcasing his most recent portraits. They are all strongly pigmented watercolours, vibrantly coloured and curiously lifelike. Eyes staring out from the screen with vibrancy.

I glance over at my own painting which looks flat and cartoonish in comparison and remind myself that this guy has committed to the craft and has honed his skills over time. I return to the home page and am about to browse some of his commissioned pieces when I see a panel advertising art classes in the top right of the screen, I click this instead. It turns out that Tim also runs a biweekly art class at the Paintery in town. This guy certainly puts the hours in. On an impulse, I fill out the registration form to attend next week's class. There's nothing like scheduling time to force commitment to a hobby.

Acrylic paint splotches are starting to crust up on my arm, so I decide to shower before I have to pick them off. As the shower steams up, I browse my bathroom cupboards for any interesting toiletries. I decide to treat my body to some exfoliation in anticipation of incidental arm brushes with Ellen. The grainy scrub is scratchy on my skin, but as I rinse it away my skin feels gloriously soft.

I dry my body and wrap the towel around my head then dash across to the bedroom. Deciding what to wear is weighted by assumptions. I shuffle the hangers back and forth looking at items scornfully. Then I touch a silky fabric and pull out a navy shirt dress. If nothing else, this feels nice. It hangs on the wardrobe door whilst I blast my hair dry. When I flip my head the right way up, my hair springs out in a dark cloud and I twist it up into a top-knot bun. I pick out some nice underwear and open the blinds a crack to let the light in whilst I apply a small amount of makeup; just enough to hide the wine flush and emphasise my eyes. I button up the dress and slip on some ballet pumps as it seems incongruous to go on a date barefoot, even if it is in my own house.

In the kitchen I check my phone which is flashing with a notification. It is from the dating app, Seth suggesting a time to meet for coffee on Tuesday. I reply to confirm that 11am works for me, then hurry to delete the thread. And in a panic, the app itself. I feel weirdly paranoid about what Ellen might think if she sees the notifications.

Ellen isn't due for another hour, but I decide to open a bottle of wine whist I prepare dinner. I feel like a fancy TV chef as I don an apron over my nice dress and lay out the ingredients on the worktop. My midriff flutters.

27

The doorbell to my flat buzzes and I spill a couple of the crudités I am laying out on a plate. I straighten up, gather my composure, and press the intercom button.

"Hello?" I ask, pretending I don't know full well that it is Ellen, enjoying being on the controlling end of the buzzer for once. She says, "It's just Ellen," casually, as though we live together, and she's forgotten her keys. Her calm voice only unsteadies my nerves further.

Through the intercom I hear her brush the door open. I quickly check my hair bun is still central, not veering off to one side. If she gets in the lift, it's less than one minute until she's at my door. Is she takes the stairs, more like two minutes. Hovering by the front door I glance over to the kitchen area wondering if there's anything else I need to prepare then realise I'm still wearing the apron and yank it off over my head. I revisit the mirror to check the bun again.

Ellen knocks. I take five seconds to breathe, then open the door. It occurs to me that I don't know whether to kiss her or just welcome her in. Ellen takes the decision out of my hands by walking straight past me as soon as the door is wide enough. I close the door slowly, collecting my thoughts, planning and re-planning my next step. When I turn, she is standing with her arms outstretched, wine in one hand, a cake box in the other.

"I brought the good stuff," she says with a grin.

"Sweet, I can put this in the fridge," I take the bottle and walk her over to the kitchen. She perches on a stool near the breakfast bar and places the box on the side.

Nerves are splitting my mental processes into two streams thought. Should I give her a tour of the place or just dish up dinner. I try to imagine that she is Riya, what would I do with Riya.

"And here's one I prepared earlier," I say in my best jaunty voice, and pull out a chilled bottle from the fridge.

"Nicely done," Ellen nods as I pour out two large glasses of white wine. We click glasses and she holds my gaze as she takes a long sip.

"So, dinner is a bit of a mixed bag," I say, casting my eyes over the multiple bowls and plates in the kitchen. "I thought the greater the choice, the higher the probability that you'd like something."

Ellen laughs a throaty noise that gives me great satisfaction. "I'm pretty easy to be honest. I love all food equally. Except for croissants, they hold a special place in my heart." I file this titbit of information away for future reference.

I start carrying plates across to the table by the window and she slips from the stool to help. I almost tell her not to, then realise she might as well; nothing more awkward than perching whilst someone ferries your dinner across the room. When we're all set up at the table, I bring over the wine bottle from the fridge remembering how quickly Ellen can neck a glass. Just as I'm about to pick up my fork, I ping back out of my seat and rummage in the supermarket bag for the candles I'd bought. Ellen watches curiously as I bring them back over and light a couple on the windowsill.

"Oooh fancy," she trills, and I blush. I realise I should have prepared this earlier, so it looked more natural, but I enjoy the atmosphere they create. Before I sit down again, I dim the lights ever so slightly. Ellen raises her eyebrows a fraction but says nothing.

"Excellent pitta!" she exclaims after her first bite, kissing her fingers dramatically. The tension melts away slightly and I fill my plate with food.

I cast around for neutral topics of conversation to ease in with "Any especially interesting sessions today?" I ask, picking my way around the stone of an olive.

She ponders this, stacking food onto her fork. "Hmmm, not today," she eyes me up. "Only one decent session this week." I smile, assuming she means me. "There was one interesting submission last night though," I think back trying to decide if this was also me, it wasn't.

"Oh yeah?" I say, trying to sound nonchalant "What was that?"

"A massage session," she says, her voice sounding disengaged. "Naturally, it turns sexual. But I need to do a bit of research before I code it."

"How much research is there to be done for a massage?

"Loads if you've never had one," she laughs.

"How have you got this far in your life without having a single massage?" I ask, amazed.

"I am just not that keen on a stranger caressing me," she picks though her food. "Besides, I am ticklish."

"Well, you are missing out!" I exclaim, "I recommend you get one ASAP. Your shoulders must be screwed from sitting at a computer so much."

Ellen looks straight at me "Doctor's orders?" there's a humour to her voice and I can't tell if it's a throwback to the first session with Riya.

"Yes, the doctor insists," I go with it. Ellen tilts one eyebrow up slightly as she reaches to pick up another pitta.

I top up the wines. As usual, Ellen seems to clear a glass in a couple of mouthfuls. I drink quickly and nervously. As she pulls apart the bread, Ellen surveys the flat. Most of the space can be seen from the table, only the bedroom and bathroom are hidden behind doors. She fixates on something in the middle of the room, and I follow her gaze; my body grows cold as I realise I have left the painting of the Virginia Howl lady in the corner to dry. But it's too late, she is already on her feet, walking over to take a closer look.

"Did you paint this?" she asks, walking up to the canvas.

"Err yes, it's supposed to be like, the um Virginia Howl book," my brain evidently can't string a sentence together under pressure.

"Kinda looks like me, doesn't it," she says peering down at it, then looking back to me.

I clear my throat, "Yeah she does have a resemblance to you." I try to be casual and force myself to carry on eating though my mouth is uncomfortably dry. Ellen's plate is already empty; I guess she eats as fast as she drinks.

"Come and tell me about your painting." Ellen takes a seat on the sofa and pats the space next to her dramatically. I carry our wine glasses over and sit at the other end of the sofa. Ellen looks more at home on my sofa than I do, I reposition myself and sip some more wine to try and appear relaxed.

"I haven't painted for years, but my friend lent me this." I reach over to the Howl book Connor lent me and open it between us. Ellen leans in, and I catch a scent of sweet shampoo as her hair hangs forward. "I just felt inspired to paint something again." I flick through the pages of the book, explaining some of the facts I found out about Virginia Howl when I read it. Her hand stops the page when we reach the strawberry blonde woman. "That's me!" she exclaims, and I laugh, impressed she sees a resemblance to what I had painted. "Except that you have done a much better job of capturing my smile," Ellen says. Comparing the two, I realise I have painted more of a smile that the sombre Howl lady.

"The serious expression doesn't suit you," I say, incited by the wine. "That professional Vie Lab persona you do. I much prefer your out of work personality."

Ellen swirls her wine and sips at the vortex "I know," she agrees. "I hate that bit, I'd much rather be the secret orchestrator, but the Professor thought it would ease people's minds if they knew who was manipulating the machinery. So, I became front of house *and* back stage, which wasn't too bad when we both worked there." She folds her arms, wine glass held loosely near her shoulder.

157

"Why doesn't he just hire someone else?" I ask, it seems like a fairly obvious decision to me.

Ellen rolls her eyes and shakes her head. "Yeah, I keep suggesting that, but he's paranoid about employing anyone else at this stage in case they pirate the software. It's his life's work. And mine, I guess. His plan is to source extra funding to take it to the next stage. This is why he's been swanning around conferences all over Europe - he's desperate to find the perfect investor."

"What is the next stage?" I ask, barely waiting for her to finish her last sentence.

Ellen grimaces, "I really shouldn't disclose anymore. I've already let you in on a lot that we've been keeping between us for a very long time."

"Well, you know you can trust me," I tell her, accidentally closing the book as I pull my knee up onto the sofa.

"Oh yeah, I know that" Ellen smiles. "You signed a contract the first time you came to the Vie Lab remember," she laughs. "Why do you think I let you stay for session one? I had to make sure you signed the form!"

"Ohh," I cover my hurt with sarcasm. "I always assumed you saw potential in me."

"Well, yes I saw some potential," she continues, then with a subtle shift, places her hand on top of mine.

"Was it my keen interest in the data?" I try to keep the flirting buoyant.

Ellen laughs again and sips her wine. "Yes that, and you're hot so that was difficult."

"Difficult?" As immodest as it is to question this clause, I want to dig for some more insights. Two glasses of wine seem to pry Ellen right open, and I want to make the most of it.

"Yeah, I couldn't decide whether to keep it professional or whether to try and fuck you." I realise my mouth is open and close it.

"Why not both?" I say, quieter than I intended.

Ellen smiles and crinkles her face "Well, it's little too late to be one hundred percent professional," she downs her wine dregs. "But I like you working with me. Livens it up a little having a colleague... of sorts."

Then she leans in to kiss me. I realise the Howl book is squashed between us and slide it to the floor. The intensity of the kiss increases, and I chance placing my hand on the top of her leg. She doesn't resist, so I slide it a little further down, then slowly to the inside of her thigh and up beneath her skirt. She takes in a breath as my fingers brush the outside of her knickers.

We are pressed together, and I feel the softness of her body leaning into me. I want her skin against mine. I want to taste her. I start to work her skirt down from her hips and she obliges. I remove her knickers slowly, enjoying the reveal of delicate freckles on her soft stomach and thighs. I lean in and am delighted by her soft gasp.

When the pleasure turns breathless, I slow. In the quiet, I slide back onto the sofa. I am about to lean in for another kiss when Ellen twists to look at her watch.

"Oh my god it's late." Her face is stained pink, and she seems suddenly hurried.

"Why don't you stay here?" I ask, bemused as she fiddles with putting her clothes back on.

"I'm really sorry, I've got to get back to Ted. I've never left him alone overnight, he'll probably be freaking out already."

All the enthusiasm I was gathering from the situation drains away. It seems weird to end the night here. But Ellen seems set on her decision. She pulls her phone from her bag up and texts for a taxi to pick her up.

"What about dessert?" I say feebly, though I know it's too late.

"You enjoy them both, seeing as how I am shooting off yet again, "she heads to the door and dons her jacket and shoes.

A jangle from her phone alerts us that the taxi is here.

"I'll text you later," she leans over and kisses me briefly on the mouth. "Thanks for a lovely evening."

I nod, smile and say goodbye, but inside a coldness creeps in.

28

A gnawing feeling of awkwardness keeps me awake. I keep checking my phone to see if Ellen has text. I even cave and text her to see if she got in, but no reply. Something didn't go right tonight. After a long time tossing and turning, unravelling the scenarios through my head, I conclude that I probably came on too strong, and the painting may have been creepy. To try and give myself closure, I get out of bed and move the painting out of the living room. It doesn't fit in the bin, so I lie it on top of the recycling box. Sleep still does not consume me fully.

In the morning, I check my phone but there are no messages from Ellen. In my compulsion to purge the flat of anything incriminating, I text Connor to say I'll post his book back today if he's in. The living room scene makes me cringe, the wine glasses on the table, the pillows on the sofa askew. Dinner plates are still out with remnants of food because I was too cross to tidy up before I crawled into bed.

My phone bleeps and my heart leaps, but when I swipe open the window, I see it's just Connor replying:

"I'm free today if you fancy a coffee? I could meet you in town in a couple of hours?"

I confirm, I need to get out of the flat and get some perspective. A message pings again.

"Sorry I didn't text to say I got home OK. Fell asleep in my clothes - absolutely shattered, mainly your fault! Thanks for dinner x."

It takes me a minute to process that it's Ellen, then all of my frustration slides away. I can forgive her for being incommunicado if the reason is post-coital shutdown. A little smug smile creeps in. Now the mess in the living room seems more romantic, but I clear it all away anyway. Tidy home, tidy mind.

Connor texts to tell me he's at Archway Cafe, a short walking distance from my flat so I head into town clutching the large Howl book. Connor is easy to spot sat in the window, reading a book. He always looks styled for a high fashion mag photoshoot. The cafe is bustling, people queuing for coffee and takeaway pastries, a handful sat at the pokey tables waiting on food. Connor doesn't notice me arriving.

"What are you reading?" I ask, to withdraw him from concentration.

"Oh hi, sorry I'm totally lost here," he stands to hug me. "It's a Spanish copy of *The Moon Eternal*. Except that my Spanish is not very good, so I think I'm missing the point. What do you want to drink?"

"I'll get them, you read your pretentious book," I say, placing the Howl book on the table next to his paperback.

"Thanks, a flat white please."

"Are you eating?" I ask, realising I haven't had any food yet.

"Oh, go on then, I'll have some boiled bananas." he laughs at my disgusted face "Trust me they're delicious! They're the only reason I come here."

The coffee shop is decorated like a beachside bar, with weathered wooden furniture and colourful fairy lights. It doesn't really fit the usually overcast skies of Manchester, but I enjoy the atmosphere, it makes me feel like I'm on holiday. A black chalk board stretches the wall behind the coffee bar, I scan the choices for brunch, but nothing jumps out at me. Connor's suggestion of boiled bananas intrigues me, so I order two servings and some coffee. A blue-haired woman in her early twenties assures me that my order will be over soon.

I re-join Connor at the table. He has abandoned his Spanish book and is now leafing through the Howl book.

What did you think of the paintings?" he asks, pausing briefly to peer at one of the portraits.

"I really like them. In fact, I was inspired to get my old art stuff out again."

Connor perks up "That's brilliant," he says. "It's such a shame when people discard their hobbies."

He's right, I almost want to lie and say I kept up sketching, but I can't actually remember the last time I drew anything before this week. Connor keeps flicking, and overleaf the strawberry blonde woman appears. I reach over to smooth the page out, noticing that there is a slight crease from where I propped it up.

"This lady was my muse," I tell him, looking intently at the picture. I'm secretly afraid that he will look into my eyes and know the truth.

"She is very striking. Artists seem to have a thing for redheads, they are a common muse."

I nod silently, still looking at the image wondering if I can remember any famous paintings of redheads, but my thoughts drift to Ellen. We are interrupted by the coffee arriving at the table.

Connor closes the book and pushes it away, then asks, "So what's new happening with you?" He takes a sip of his small coffee.

I put my cup down and shake my head. "Hm, not much." My usual response. Not much *has* changed the past year since I got the job at the university. Apart from the Vie Lab, but nothing could be said about that.

"What about that date the other day," Connor asks, eyebrows sneaking upwards.

I smile, the relationship with Ellen had been too confusing to explain to Riya, but Connor didn't know the first thing about her, so I could edit the story for him.

"Oh yes it was good. We met through a mutual friend from work," I begin, not a massive lie, though Riya was hardly friends with Ellen. "And we've been on a few dates now." At least one of these has been romantic so I don't feel bad pluralising the word date.

"Do they work at the University too?" Connor asks. This is harder to explain, as I'm technically not sure if Ellen works at the University.

"She works in town," the boiled bananas arrive at our table, laying in bowls of thick treacle sauce. Connor is wide-eyed, but I have to take a minute to laugh at the situation.

"So how serious are we talking? Like have you done anything naughty?" He whispers, eyebrows arched, taking a sticky bite out of his food.

I lean in to whisper. "It's probably easier to ask what we *haven't* done." He coughs a little in surprise.

"Oh my god Nicole! I'm impressed. I did not expect this at all, especially from you. No offence! It's just that you're like my most strait-laced friend. I can't believe you're having a sexual awakening at twenty-nine! God, I feel like a Stepford housewife in comparison."

I laugh as he rolls his eyes "Come on, what you have with Rick is wonderful," I retort.

"Doesn't stop me from wanting to live vicariously through single people. Tell me all the details."

I take a first bite of my banana bowl, "Oh my gosh you're right, this is amazing," I tell him through a claggy, sweet mouthful. When I have swallowed the dessert, I continue. "There's not much more to tell," I lean in dramatically. "That I can disclose at a coffee shop." Connor is loving the drama. "She took me to dinner, I made dinner for her at my place, we get on really well."

"Sounds great!" Connor enthuses. "And you seem much more excited about this than other dates I've heard you describe. Maybe she's the one?" I blush. It seems absurd to think of Ellen as a soulmate when I have only known her a few weeks, but I enjoy the description. It makes the relationship seem more official than it currently feels.

165

I enjoy spending the rest of brunch disclosing small but interesting details about the time spent with Ellen, managing to refrain from slipping any details of the Vie Lab, or name dropping just in case he knows of her. Then Connor fills me in on his plans for him and Rick to buy a bigger house so that they have space when his family visit. And perhaps for a future family. In terms of relationship progression, Connor and Rick feel lightyears ahead. I cannot fathom deciding to spend my life with someone or shed my independence for a family. But I enjoy the stories.

When I leave Connor to walk back to my flat, I check my phone. I have a missed call and text message from Ellen which simply reads:

"Ring me ASAP."

My buzz instantly burns out.

29

I decide to wait until I am back home before calling Ellen; the brevity of her message unsettles me. As soon as I get back, I kick off my shoes, slam the front door and dial her number before sitting down on the sofa whilst the phone rings through. My hands are shaking, I hope my voice doesn't.

"Hi Nicole," Ellen answers after what feels like endless ringing. I can hear traffic noise, so I assume she's outside.

"Hey, I just got your message. What's up?" I try to match her neutral tone, but my voice breaks slightly.

"I was just wondering if you are free this evening?" I want to be excited by this proposition, but something in her voice sounds different. Dread builds in my stomach.

"Is something wrong, you seem a bit off?"

"No, I'm fine. The reason I ask is that Eric - Professor McAllister - wants to meet you. He's back in town briefly and wants to do dinner tonight."

"Why does he want to meet me?" I ask, uneasy at the tone of her voice.

"I mentioned you to him, just discussing Vie Lab new clients," my heart sinks - new clients? "But I think he was a bit annoyed that I didn't screen him past you. He has full sight of the other clientele so..." her voice trails out; I sense there is something else coming. "And I think I dropped myself in it a bit," she continues. "Eric is a very perceptive man and perhaps I was a little too complimentary about you." She lets out a long sigh, but I feel a tiny bit pleased receiving this second-hand compliment. "So, I think he wants to check there's nothing weird going on. He is quite *overprotective*." Silence hangs for a moment as I process this.

"Overprotective of you or the Vie Lab?"

"The lab," she says quickly, "Well, I guess me too. He's always been a bit paranoid that I might get poached by another researcher."

"Okay, well let's just reassure him that nothing *weird* is going on. I am not trying to poach you, am I?" I hope she reads into my flirty joke, but she skips over it.

"Phew, thank you." she lets out a long breath, there is genuine relief in her voice. "I don't think I'll lose my job, you know given that it's pretty much a one-woman show at the moment. I just think he wants to check everything is OK," she seems to be trying to convince herself.

"Yeahhh, it's just a client relations dinner," I say, as though I know what that means.

"Yeah?" Ellen seems to take comfort in my justification, so I make a confirmation noise and she continues, "Well, let's see what happens. Is eight o'clock, OK? I suggested that we meet at the fancy tapas place near Victoria. The Professor loves the sangria there, so we might be able to loosen him up a tad," she lets out a tight laugh and my anxiety starts to swell again. I'm not used to Ellen seeming insecure and it is unsettling.

"Perfect, see you there," I say and am about to add on a question about dress code when I realise Ellen has already hung up. It doesn't matter too much because my wardrobe is limited, but the omission of goodbye is jarring.

◆ ◆ ◆

I plan to arrive at the restaurant slightly late, so I can be the last one to the table. It seems easier than risking being alone with the Professor without Ellen. However, when I arrive at 8:10, uncomfortably late for me, it is just Ellen sat at the table. I walk over towards her and my heart sinks seeing how uneasy she is. Her body is tight, elbows fixed to her chest, right hand at her face pulling at her bottom lip, eyes trained on the window.

"Sorry I am late." I say, startling her out of her fixation.

"Oh, thank god I was worried you weren't coming," she doesn't stand to hug me, but I appreciate that is probably inappropriate. "Eric is always late, so I expected that."

"Shall we get some sangria?" I'm thinking a glass before he arrives might ease the nerves a little. Ellen nods, then flicks her eyes back to the window, presumably looking out for the Professor.

I order some wine then try to engage Ellen in some light chat to take her mind off the situation, "What have you been up to today?"

"Hmm?" she says but doesn't turn to look at me. I realise that she's not going to relax until he arrives, so I try to establish some normality for myself. I tell her about my meeting with Connor and the things he told me about the artist's obsession with redheads, thinking she might enjoy this, but she doesn't seem to be registering anything I am saying. Then suddenly her face changes entirely and she stands up, looking over my shoulder. I stand up automatically and turn to face an older man arriving at the table. He has thick grey hair coiffed back from his face, and a narrow angular face.

"You must be Nicole?" he says extending a slim-fingered hand for me to shake. I grasp it firmly. "I am indeed, and you are Professor Eric McAllister?" A broad smile breaks across his face and he says, "Oh please, just Eric thank you."

He doesn't shake Ellen's hand but says hello and smiles warmly as he takes a seat beside her at the table. A brown briefcase is tucked beside his chair leg, and he lays his folded neck scarf over the handle. It feels like I am about to be interviewed by the two of them, except that Ellen is showing the nerves of a candidate. Eric seems to be completely at ease, oblivious to the tension emanating from Ellen. The pitcher of sangria arrives, and I apologise for not waiting.

"Perfect timing," he says, dismissing my comment and pouring us each a glass.

The Professor takes his time perusing the menu without further comment, as relaxed as if he was in the company of old friends. I wish Ellen would break the ice, but she seems to be withdrawn from her usual role as leader in the presence of Eric. I debate interrupting the silence with some polite chit-chat, but Eric saves me the trouble.

"Ellen tells me you are a psychologist?" he asks, closing his menu and clasping his hands together atop, mock therapist pose.

"Yes, I work on cognitive dissonance disorder, building neural models to try and find patterns to help sufferers align their conflicting beliefs and behaviours," I take a sip of wine, my throat suddenly dry like I am indeed at a job interview.

"What sorts of beliefs?" He asks, and Ellen seems to tune into the conversation at this point.

I hesitate. Even though I know so many case studies, his intense blue eyes are off putting, and I can only reel off a generic example under the pressure.

"Erm, well for example if you think you are a good person, but then do something immoral and your brain cannot comprehend it, so you deny the behaviour." I don't take appropriate breaths in explaining this.

Eric glances at Ellen and nods, a bemused smile on his face. "Ellen said you'd done some work with neuroimaging." I hear this as a question though there is no inflection in the sentence.

"Yes, this past year I've been working quite a bit at the neuroimaging centre. There are a few different neuro teams at the University. My friend Riya -,"

"Ah yes, Dr Cooper," the Professor interrupts and throws a glance to Ellen, who doesn't return it. "Her research really stood out to us," Eric's gaze returns steadily to me. "What happened to her?"

I don't know whether he is addressing me or Ellen, so I say, "She's still working at the University."

Ellen cuts in, her voice low. "Dr Cooper attended a couple of sessions but was not interested in contributing to the research."

"That is a shame." Eric says, nosing his sangria like a fine wine then drinking half the glass in one slug. I wonder if Ellen picked this habit up from him. "But Ellen tells me you've been helping her out?" the tone of his voice is a tad patronising, but I that might just be my paranoid lens. After spending most of my career assisting someone else's research to get where I am, it burns to be assumed someone's assistant.

"The research is very interesting; I was keen to find out more about your work." I play to the fact I know this project was once entirely his. His polite smile broadens.

"Yes, it is very interesting, I've spent most of my life working on this project. The first ten years were pre-alpha phase, and I was the sole researcher. Ellen came in at alpha phase. Now, five years on we're at beta testing phase and it has been very interesting to see how it has been received by our panel." Ellen is nodding in agreement, but her continued silence is unsettling. I feel like I'm about to be fired or dumped and she doesn't want to be responsible.

"Though admittedly, I haven't heard much feedback in person. Ellen usually reports back to me. I've been very busy this year trying to secure the legacy of the project. We can't remain a two-man operation forever." I wonder whether Ellen is insulted by his casual use of the word *man*, but she doesn't react.

The waiter comes over to take our food order, and when he leaves Ellen finally jumps into the conversation.

"I've been telling Eric how popular the project has become," she fixes her gaze on me, though I feel the message is directed at the Professor. "There's not enough time to plan and write the number of scenarios required any more. Beta testing clients are into it in a big way, I can't do a customer management role as well as a research job." She seems to relax slightly after pouring this out.

"Yes, I agree," Eric ponders a moment. "And I am looking into a solution. We nearly have the software at release candidate stage, and the scenarios library is very well developed so soon we'll be set for gold." I assume he is still talking in software lingo, so I press for clarity.

"What does being set for gold mean?"

He interlaces his fingers loosely and looks at them, as though trying to decide how to possibly explain this concept to a novice.

"Technically it means live release of software to the public, but I feel in our case it might mean something different. I'm not convinced that gen pop is ready to deal with this just yet." He turns in his chair to face towards Ellen, "But we can talk about the boring business stuff later."

Eric finishes the end of his wine as the food starts to arrive, so he orders another pitcher of sangria. I am aware that I have barely touched mine, and Ellen also seems to clock her glass, so we tip a few sips back.

I decide to drill down on Vie Lab history, as the Professor seems to enjoy talking about it. A little more openly than Ellen I note.

"How did you first get the idea for the project?" I ask as Eric picks his way through a small bowl of olives.

"It wasn't really one idea," he says. "More of a series of elaborations on different projects coming together as one thing. As the technology got better, so did the experience." He pauses to spit an olive stone into his hand and disposes it on his side plate. Clearly, he is used to holding the attention of his audience. "At first, I developed training simulations with the aim of marketing it to the military. As I am sure you're aware, they have a large research and development budget, so you can set yourself up quite nicely as a computer scientist there if you want to. However, over time I got more and more attached to the project and when I retired, I took the idea - and Ellen - with me." He looks at her fondly, but she continues to poke her fork around a plate of patatas bravas. The level of sangria in his glass is quickly depleting, and I feel a pressure to keep up with him.

"When we got to the beta phase, we let participants suggest ideas for the scenarios. "He leans in towards me, cupping his wine glass and almost whispering, "And who'd have guessed that eighty percent of them were *intimate.* It turns out that people really are driven by sex," he laughs to himself as though there's a private joke and leans back. It occurs to me in a horrible flash of realisation the he has probably read my scenario request. I berate myself for thinking that would be something kept between Ellen and I. Eric continues, oblivious to my rising flush. "By the end of the second year of testing we'd written several hundred scenarios, but we realised we could reuse snippets of different ideas. There was lots of overlap. People are not so different when you strip them down to their primal fantasies."

"What about non-sexual ones - what were they like?" I ask hoping to avoid any recognition of my own preferences. I look at Ellen, encouraging her involvement, and hoping the Professor redirects his attention.

"Oh, you know, sports-related, living out bits from famous films, anti-gravity-"

Eric interrupts her "Do you remember the man who just wanted a room full of cats for an hour, that was an easy one!"

Ellen nods a small smile and goes back to her food. It's so strange seeing her withdraw like this. It is rapidly depleting my respect for her. I try to bring her back:

"Any really weird ones?" I ask her.

She thinks for a moment, then in a low voice says, "There was an older lady who wanted to be squashed by a body builder." They both start giggling, "I shouldn't laugh, I mean it's personal preference, and it was actually really hard to monitor how far to take it you know without overdoing it, but my god did she enjoy it!"

Some of the tension seems to dissipate after the laughter dies down. The Professor finishes his glass of wine and leans back so he can survey us both in a shorter turn of the head. The way he is looking at Ellen makes me feel a little jealous. It seems different than professional affection, but I know better than to press it. I recognise that my personal interest in Ellen is biasing my perceptions.

The food is cleared, and dessert menus brought to us. The Professor looks at his watch and says, "Please excuse the brevity of my visit, but I really must be going." Ellen's face falls and she presses her lips together. He withdraws some money from his wallet, more than enough for the meal and puts it on the table. I start to refuse this excessive contribution, but he insists we continue the wine and food without him.

"Ellen, I will see you tomorrow. Ladies, goodnight," he says and swiftly exits, leaving his dessert menu open in his place.

"Do you think he is reassured that I am not here to pirate your software?" I try to break the tension, but Ellen seems fixed in her anxiety. "He didn't seem to suspect that we... you know, crossed the line," I lean in towards her, but she leans back.

"I don't know about that," she replies, her eyes flicking to the door. "He is very perceptive. But also, very good at being polite. I think he was choosing to reveal what he wanted to for the sake of the situation,"

"So, what's the problem, why are you being so uptight?" I press.

She sighs. "Ugh I don't know; I haven't seen him for a while and things can be a bit funny between us," she slides her teeth across her lip, "it was a bit weird for a while."

"Weird how?" A dryness in my throat catches the words.

"Weird as in..." she tucks one hand deep into her hair, "I had a crush on him for a while."

My stomach drops. "But he's like double your age!" I exclaim.

"Oh god I know, I don't really want to talk about it, I was young. Younger. Nothing happened anyway, it just meant Eric grew more and more detached from the project," she trails off but the question of why still hangs in the air. My face displays this. "I'd rather forget about it," she pleads.

I desperately want to know the details, but I get the sense that Ellen would not appreciate a grilling, so I drop it. The questions will plague me later but it's not worth upsetting her now.

The mood has definitely darkened, and neither of us want dessert so we call for the bill and a taxi. Ellen offers to drop me off at my place, but I say I want to walk. There's nothing more disappointing than being dropped off at your own house instead of going home with someone after dinner.

30

The night-time air clears some of the alcohol buzz from my head. I arrive home exhausted, so I head straight to the bathroom to get ready for bed. As I am setting the alarm on my phone, a message pings through from Ellen.

"I'm sorry about tonight. I know it wasn't that fun for you, but I wanted Eric to meet you. You are a great asset to the project, and I want him to see it."

I feel confused, the message reads like a colleague has written it. I can't face another night of debating our relationship status with myself, so I decide to call her out on it.

"I'm really not sure what you want from me Ellen. Do you see me as a work partner or romantic partner?" I reply.

I see the dotted lines in the message box come to life, indicating that she is typing. I cradle my phone waiting. Then, a reply:

"Why not both? I'm sorry I was so weird tonight. I was just worried that Eric would jump to conclusions about us. You're not just a client testing the software."

I want to feel relieved by this response. She has fulfilled both my desire to be attractive to her and be involved in the project, but the matter-of-factness of the message doesn't put me at ease. As I lie there considering a tactful reply, I fall asleep.

◆ ◆ ◆

Oddly realistic dreams plague me through the night, and I am woken by a pain my back. I reach down to touch it and find the cold metal of my phone poking into my spine. I retrieve it and see that I have had several messages from Ellen, starting with a message half an hour after I the last one I read:

"I'm sorry Nicole I should have explained all this in person back at your place. Sometimes I forget that I haven't told you how I feel, I assume you know x."

And then another 15 minutes after this:

"Can I see you tomorrow evening? X."

I feel harsh for not replying but remember that she had me in the same situation not long ago. It definitely makes sense to meet in person to talk, instant messaging absorbs so much of the personality from conversations. I reply:

"Sorry, I fell asleep before your messages came through. Sure, I will come to yours tonight. What time will you be in?"

I'm surprised to see that the typing icon starts to move as she types a reply.

"I'll be back about 6 tonight, so come around 6:30? I will order Chinese food x."

Now I feel more excited. That's more like a date reply, and earlier than I anticipated. I reply to confirm I will be there and drag myself out of bed.

I make marmalade on toast for breakfast and sit with my laptop. The local news website tells me that the Science Museum has appointed its first ever woman as Director; I click through to read more. A banner ad pops up on the page to tell me that there is an exhibition about neurophysiology on this weekend. I must have missed a work email about this whilst on leave. A little trip to the museum might be a good way to spend the day.

Arriving at the grand brick museum brings a wave of nostalgia; a reminder of my pre-PhD days when I would browse for pleasure, enjoying the quiet prickle of energy of as I drifted around the rooms. A sign directs me to the neurophysiology exhibition set up in one of the smaller rooms, a mix of scientific miscellany and old framed books. Glass cabinets displaying models of the brain and nervous system standing next to Perspex containers of preserved specimens. No one else is browsing this section so my footsteps echo as I pace the room. I lean in to read musings of philosophers in their golden notebooks, and step back to view full sized comparisons of primate brains. When I reach the far corner, my interest is piqued. There is a mini presentation about neurostimulation, and in a small glass cube lies a headband similar to the spectator band of the Vie Lab. I rustle in my bag to pull out my notebook.

"That's the actual prototype." A voice breaks the silence.

"Bloody hell!" I curse, forgetting to keep my voice low. I turn and see Professor Eric McAllister standing in the middle of the room, his hands clasped behind his back and a bemused expression on his face.

"Apologies for startling you," he says, rocking silently from toe to heel.

"How long have you been here?" I ask, gathering my wits and my breath.

"Only just popped in," he says, eyebrows slightly raised. "Nice to see you taking an interest in the exhibition."

"Yes, well it's always good to remind yourself of the history..." I trail off, not entirely confident this is a good answer.

"And look to the future," he says, nodding at the headband "I have a friend at the museum, he asked if I could contribute this piece to bring it into the 21st century. I didn't think it would get that much traction, and I was right," he laughs from his nose. "But still, it's good to see a few people engaged."

The Professor turns on his heels and walks softly towards the door, I watch him wondering whether he will leave as vaguely as he arrived. Just before the exit he turns and says, "Nice to see you, Nicole. I'm late for a meeting, but I'm sure I'll see you soon." His eyes light with a brief glint of amusement, then he is gone.

When I leave the museum, I have a message from Ellen.

"If you're free then I have some time off this afternoon at the lab - Professor is out all day."

I reply to ask if now is good, I'm a 20-minute walk away. Thirty mins if I stop for coffee and sandwiches. She confirms that 30 with lunch in tow would be perfect.

I pick up a couple of hummus wraps and Americanos and head to the Vie Lab. Ellen greets me with an uncertain smile. Not the intimate recognition I crave, but better than a professional chill. She leads me through to the control room, where she seems to loosen up.

"How hungry are you?" she asks, her smile broadening.

"Hm, I'm not starving," I reply.

"Do you fancy trial running my new massage scenario," she asks barely before I've finished.

"Yeah, sure," I shrug. It seems rude to turn down a free massage.

"Excellent, thanks!" Ellen sits down at one of the computers and begins tapping "I read that you should have a massage on an empty stomach, so this is perfect."

I shed my layers and place my lunch next to my bag on the chair. Ellen turns briefly to encourage me to enter the room.

I oblige and depress the handle of the door. Almost as soon as the door closes behind me, the lights click off and then back on. No formalities now it seems.

The room now felt much smaller, a very intimate space stacked with decorative wall hangings and draped fabric. A warm light was cast from multiple candles and a lamp in the corner. A soft knocking comes from the corner of the room, and a man enters from the doorway.

"Good afternoon, I am Jay," the man is short and stocky with a gentle voice. "I have you in for a Swedish massage?" He says, straight to the point. I nod. "OK, remove all clothing and lie on the table please, beneath the towel," he closes the door behind him quietly. I fold my jeans and t-shirt and place them onto a chair at the side of the massage table. I try not to think of Ellen in the other room as I remove my bra and knickers. I am under the towel in no time. Jay re-enters the room and turns on some gentle woodwind music.

"Please try to relax." He folds the towel halfway down my back and drizzles warm oil across my back, distributing it across my back with warm hands. The sensation is very soothing, and I find myself relaxing into it. His strong hands feel good smoothing out tensions in my neck and back. When the whole of my back feels warm and loose, he folds the towel back further so that now it was only covering my feet. I tense slightly at the exposure. But after the initial shock of having my legs and buttocks stroked by a stranger subsides, I start to relax again.

"Is this pressure OK?" he asks as he steps the massage up to a slightly deeper tissue. I nod my face in the head-cradle. His strong, soft hands feel good pushing against the tight muscles in my calves and thighs. Jay circles the bed and, without even touching my body, manoeuvres himself into a kneeling position straddling my lower back. There is a brief pause as he re-oils his hands and my body yearns for his warm touch again. He restarts by placing his fingertips at the base of my spine and lowering his whole hands onto my lower back. He pushes down, and the pressure intensifies, but the release is glorious. He repeats this several times, then on the final press, leans forward to push his hand up and over my buttocks. He pauses here, squeezing and releasing the flesh in his hands. It is oddly erotic having his strong hands knead the muscles in my backside.

I become aware of a tingling in my crotch and tense my legs together. Jay seamlessly moves to a long massage stroke up and down the backs of my thighs. The feeling was bordering on tickling, and I must have tensed up again because Jay whispers, "Try to release the tension Nicole," gently sliding his palms to the inside of my thighs, drawing them apart slightly. He continues with the long, fluid strokes along the length of my thighs, now his thumbs grazed the inside of my thighs. My heart rate quickens as I remember Ellen mentioning a sexual element of the session in development. And then his fingers confirm the progression.

A jolt runs through me, then a ripple of pleasure. I can't bring myself to relax entirely into the situation, but the growing tension is delicious. I breathe and allow the feeling to cascade across my whole body. Jay stays in sync and, on release, grows still. He draws the towel back up over my back and presses off the excess oil.

When this closing procedure is finished, he whispers, "I will leave you to get yourself ready," and quietly leaves the room. I lay still for a while. A combination of relaxed muscles, post-orgasm stupor and confusion. I possibly fall asleep because I am jolted back to realty by Ellen's voice over the intercom. "Hello Nic, it's Ellen. The scenario is due to end shortly so are you happy to come out?" Embarrassment shakes me awake and I am in my clothes and out of the door in no time.

I feel my face flushing in the control room, but Ellen is too busy closing down the machines to notice.

"How was it?" she asks.

"Err yes, very relaxing," I reply with an awkward laugh.

"Convincing?" she asks, turning to face me.

"Yes. Well, I've only had one professional massage before, but it didn't end quite like that." Ellen's eyes narrow slightly, but a smile grows on her lips.

"What about non-professional?" she presses.

I flinch, then boldly say "Sure, they were usually sexual."

"Exactly," she replies and turns back to the computer. I sit next to her and pick up my wrap I notice hers is also untouched.

"Not hungry?" I ask, poking the sandwich next to her mouse.

"Oh, yes. I was just a little busy orchestrating," she smiles but continues looking at the screen.

I take a hearty bite from my lunch. "So how much of the session is improv?" I ask, trying to sound casual.

Ellen also unwraps her sandwich, and swings round to face me. "Depends on the case," she says through a mouthful of bread. "Some people are more predictable than others."

"Where do I fall on the spectrum?" I cannot resist.

"You are harder work," she takes another bite. I return her playful smile.

Ellen's phone starts to buzz on the desk. She casts an eye to it then swears, dropping her wrap back to the table.

"Hi Eric," my heart sinks hearing the Professor's name. Ellen nods at the phone a couple of times then says "Sure, see you soon."

She returns her phone to the desk but doesn't pick up her sandwich again. Through a plaintive expression she says, "I'm really sorry, but you need to leave."

"What, why?" my appetite drops off.

"The Professor is heading over here to talk me through something important and it's going to look weird if you're here out of hours."

I can tell she is as disappointed as I feel so I don't argue.

"You owe me dinner," I say, trying to pick up the mood. Ellen gives me a half smile.

"Absolutely." she replies, standing up to encourage my movement. I follow suit, packing up my belongings and heading to reception.

"See you soon," I say, heading towards the door.

"Please don't be cross," Ellen says softly, following me out.

"I'm not cross," I say, but it's hard to place exactly what I am.

Ellen leans over and kisses me, full on the lips.

"Tomorrow night, if you're free, then dinner is on me," she says, a forlorn cast to her eyes.

I nod then turn. Afraid that if I utter any words, they will come out unpleasantly weak.

31

Monday drags. I struggle to reengage with the barrage of electronic messages my desk subjects me to, so I take myself to the library for most of the day to do some lecture prep. After hours engrossed in papers about cognitive psychology, I am roused by my phone vibrating. Riya is checking we are still on for lunch. I check my watch; it is in fact lunch time. I reply hastily as I dash out of the door.

Riya is waiting for me outside The Coffee Machine and the predictability feels reassuring after the past week. Though I am keen to dive straight in with my questions about the Vie Lab partnership, Riya gets in there first with stories of her weekend date. She is smitten with Sal and gets increasingly excited as she talks about him. The conversation dominates most of the lunchtime, with details that go beyond what I feel you should disclose about a person, but I indulge her because I empathise. Eventually, Riya remembers the text I sent her at the weekend.

"So, what are all these dates you mentioned? Sounds like someone got suddenly lucky in love?"

I remember that I said I'd meet Seth tomorrow; Riya would appreciate knowing that I took up her advice about online dating, so I force a coy smile and tell her.

"I did what you suggested - I downloaded the app and trawled through the results."

"Oooh was there much talent?" she asks.

I laugh "Barely, though I did have a few messages," not technically a lie, I did have several messages that I didn't reply to. "I've got a date tomorrow actually."

She claps her hands in exaggerated excitement. "Ohhh yesss," she hisses "What does he do?"

Weird how everyone immediately wants to know where everyone works. "He works at the Uni," I whip my head around to make sure he's not sat behind me. The coffee shop is still pretty quiet, but even so I drop my voice just in case anyone overhears. "Research on stem cells I think."

Suddenly Riya's excited face drops, "Oh please tell me it's not Seth Guntree," she whispers.

"Why what's wrong with him?" I ask, almost defensively.

"If it is him, I wouldn't bother. The guy is completely unhinged, well after a few drinks at least. Alcohol seems to shed his protective layers of normality."

I frown, "You think everyone is unhinged Ri, remember Bill? He never did anything weird, but you had a 'gut feeling' about him," I poke my fork towards her in a joke pitchfork action. "Stop demonising everyone."

"No seriously, Seth-" she drops her voice right down, causing me to lean in closer which I am sure she is just doing for dramatic effect, "he's odd I'm sure of it. I met him a few times when I first started online dating. He cried on our first *and* second date." I suppress a jibe, I want to ask what she did to him, but her face isn't humorous "Then on the last date - yes I gave him one more chance," she interjects seeing my raised eyebrows. "He got quickly drunk and told me how he'd cheated on all his previous girlfriends. He somehow thought he was the victim in the story."

"Yeah, OK he sounds a little odd," I tell her, setting my face to one of concern. "I think I'll rain check that date," secretly relieved that I can bail without guilt. Riya has nearly finished her food and I panic we won't have time to discuss the Vie Lab, so I run straight into a new conversation without giving her chance to reply.

"Luckily, I have another date tonight," Riya's eyes widen, but her mouth is full of sandwich, so she doesn't say anything. "It's with Ellen," I continue. Riya's eyes narrow and she swallows.

"Oh, is that a *date* or is it an appointment at the ... bookbinders." she remembers to keep it anonymous but it's not very convincing if anyone is listening to us.

"Yes, dinner at hers. And we had dinner at the weekend. Though that was with her boss too." Now Riya is interested "You met the Professor?" she exclaims, "Oooh what's he like?"

"He's... an interesting character. He gives off an intense energy; a weird mix of intellectual superiority and genuine curiosity."

"What does he look like? Please tell me he has wild, white professor hair?"

I laugh, shaking my head, "Nope, not at all. His hair is very much groomed. He's a bit of a silver fox actually."

Riya's jaw drops open.

"I bet you wish you hadn't passed up the opportunity to work with him now, don't you?" I say and her face crumples up, confused.

"Work with him?" she asks.

"Yeah, on the project, isn't that why you were invited in the first place?" I'm doubting whether I've remembered what Ellen had said correctly now.

"Oh no, they just said they needed testers for the lab, and I was invited because of my links to the university. I think it was easier for them to get ethics that way or something? But aside from my booked sessions I haven't done anything more," she starts to tidy up the rubbish from her lunch.

"I think they imagined that you'd get more involved." I tell her, looking for any validation of what the Professor had said.

"Hmm I don't know so," she shrugs her shoulders. "To be honest I haven't really got time at the moment," she looks at her watch. "I should really be getting back now. Let me know how it goes tonight with Ellen."

She smiles, but I get the impression she doesn't have high hopes so isn't making a big deal. I mirror her in stacking my packaging on a tray and walking to the bins. I hope that by our next meeting I have something more substantial to tell her.

As we part ways, I check my phone and see that I have a message from Ellen.

"Can you leave early today at all? The Professor wants to show you something."

I thank myself for getting into work earlier that day, at a push I can probably leave at 4. I tell her this and ask what it is he wants me to see. I feel giddy with anticipation waiting for her reply. Finally, as I get back to my desk, she messages.

"A new scenario he has written. Something different apparently. But he loves a dramatic reveal, so I think having another audience member would be fun for him. Or maybe he sees your potential."

◆◆◆

My afternoon tasks feel grey and pointless; I can barely contain myself to the office for the next three hours. To kill some time, I download the dating app again and reply to the last message from Seth to say I can't make the coffee meeting tomorrow. I lie and say I am swamped with work. I don't bother suggesting an alternative time, hoping he might get the hint. From what I have heard about online dating, it's fairly normal to flake out on dates anyway.

I open some documents that I need to work on, but my mind continually wanders back to the experience of this evening. I wonder whether I am expected to be an audience member, or an active player in the Professor's mystery scenario.

32

I arrive at Ryan's Bookbinding dead on 4:30pm and am promptly admitted upstairs. Ellen is stood at reception, and, smiling, guides me through to the control room where the Professor is sat drinking a cup of coffee. He places the cup down, precariously close to the keyboard, and ushers me in.

"Hello again Nicole, so pleased you could join us on such short notice." He stands up, "I won't beat around the bush, I have an exciting new development and I want you to be the first people to see it in action," he smiles at us in turn, evidently basking in the glory of our undivided attention. "And of course, your expertise and opinion will be most appreciated."

He slides back into the chair in front of the terminals and begins clacking away at the keyboard, pausing to sip his coffee as a series of numbers being to populate the screen. It is strange seeing someone else sitting in Ellen's chair.

I glance at Ellen, but her attention is on Eric.

"OK, you know the drill, remove any items you don't want to be burdened with in the suite," he says, eyes still fixed on his screen.

"Which of us are you talking to?" Ellen interrupts, a note of annoyance in her voice.

"Oh sorry, I mean both of you," he swings around in his chair, almost whimsically. "This is my latest development! I've finally figured out how to make the programme respond to two brain processes at once," he is beaming, but Ellen is scowling.

"Eric, I thought we said this would never be an option?" her voice comes out raised, but she tones it down mid-sentence.

"Yes, I think we did say that initially, but that was many years ago and technology has come a long way." The Professor seems unnaturally relaxed, reclining in the chair "Do you remember that conference I went to in Utrecht? Well, I attended a talk on neural mapping and differential brain wave frequencies, and it just clicked! If we just tune different receptors into the individual brain waves, then we can isolate people from one another."

"And have you tried this out with subjects yet?" Ellen asks impatiently.

"That's the plan!" Eric smiles and raises his eyebrows at Ellen, then clicks his fingers. "Ah yes, it is probably sensible to fill out these participant briefing forms, as a formality. Given that it is a slightly different program and all that."

We both stand stock still in front of him, unsure how to react. He is so assured by his idea that it seems he hasn't considered that we might not want to take part. Deep down, I actually *do* want to experience a multiplayer lab with Ellen, but her hesitance is unsettling me. She does not accept the form he tries to hand over.

"No Eric, think about it. The programme feeds off reflexive brain impulses, any potential crossover could be dangerous."

He clearly does not appreciate being challenged on the idea, and his smile drops. "Ellen do you honestly think I haven't considered that? Of course, I have. I've spent countless hours working on the dual-frequency monitor and I can assure you that the chance of interference is minute, and even if it was present would be unnoticeable given the barrage of other stimuli."

Ellen folds her arms defiantly but doesn't seem to have any further argument up her sleeve. I take one of the forms to fill in, wondering whether the crossover of brain waves would mean I could theoretically read Ellen's mind. I try not to consider whether I'd like that or not. She doesn't fill in one of the forms but does allow the Professor to usher her towards the door to the lab without any further debate.

"Just promise me that you'll reset it as soon as we say so if things get out of hand," she says before stepping over the threshold.

"Of course!" he assures her, closing the door behind us. She seems less trusting of him than I would have expected after so long working together, her face is pinched and anxious. The Professor's voice comes into the room from overhead.

"OK ladies can you hear me? You both know the drill; the lights will dip as the programme resets. *End game* signals that you want to leave the Vie Lab. Ready?"

I nod and look to Ellen for her reaction, but the lights have already shut off. My stomach drops in anticipation. As my eyes grow accustomed to the brightening room, I see that we are stood in an empty bar. The room seems far more detailed than normal, Ellen appears to be marvelling at this illusion too.

"How did you expand the stimuli boundaries?" she asks, presumably to the Professor, but no reply is received.

"Pretty impressive!" I say enthusiastically to fill the silence.

With no indication that anything is about to happen, we simply stand an observe the room. The walls are painted a dark navy blue, a large semi-circular black table frames the bar in the corner, and a handful of matching bistro tables fill the floor space. Ellen is walking towards one of the tables, so I follow her. I pull out the chair, and as I do the chair flickers to a lighter colour and then back to black.

"Did you see that?" Ellen exclaims pointing to the chair. I nod "That chair just got darker right? Just for a split second?" Ellen casts her gaze to the one-way windows in the wall.

"Lighter I think," I reply, but Ellen is already speaking to the Professor.

"Eric, I think there's a glitch in the code, can you look into it please?" Ellen says, barely masking her irritation. Again, we receive a silent reply. She sighs and sits in the chair.

I seat myself opposite her and look at her strained expression. She doesn't seem to be able to relax. I reach over to touch one of her arms in comfort, but she quickly snatches it away. After a few minutes of sitting quietly, Ellen takes a long breath in, closes her eyes and exhales slowly and loudly.

"OK," she says finally. "How long are we doing this for?" Her eyes dart to the wall again then back to me. In the second that Ellen's gaze meets mine, a dizzying flip of perception occurs. The face on Ellen's body switches to an image of my own face. A screaming version of my face. I touch my mouth, I am screaming, and so is Ellen, through my face. We both push away from the table and tip our chairs over in unison. Hot tears spring to my eyes with the rush of adrenaline, and my vision clouds.

"What the hell was that?" I ask unable to control the panic in my voice.

Ellen shouts over me "End game!" Nothing happens. "I said *end game* Eric!" Her voice splits with emotion and the lights drop. My heart rate starts to slow down, and I quickly wipe away the tears in the darkness.

The Professor opens the door to the control room, and I have to control the fear in my body urging me to run towards the light.

"What the hell was that, Eric?" Ellen shouts, echoing my words.

"I'm sorry, I don't follow what you mean," he replies, eyebrows creasing his brow.

"There was a major glitch or something." Ellen continues, her voice still shrill. "When I looked at Nicole it was like she was wearing my face. And when I screamed, the sound came out of her mouth - did you not see this? Did you have the frequency band on?"

"I did have the band on, but no I cannot say I saw this - and Nicole did you observe the same effect?" he asks, a professional tone guiding his voice.

"Yes, well except that it was my face instead of Ellen." He nods sympathetically, though I realise my answer seems silly and our reaction seems exaggerated given his response.

"Hmm, I see," he says, and sits back at the terminal. "I did not read any error reports or glitches in the code," he scrolls through boxes of text on the screen. "But perhaps there was some interference across the transmitters."

"See, this is what we said would happen," Ellen sighs deeply. "It's too risky."

"Well no, the risk is actually quite minimal, even if the likelihood is higher than anticipated. It's hardly a dangerous effect, is it?"

"It was pretty horrifying to see my screaming face on Nicole's body!" Ellen looks like she is getting riled up again. Her efforts to change the professor's mind don't seem to be working.

"Nothing a little tinkering can't fix I'm sure," he smiles, and leans back in his chair again. "Did you like the expansion?" He asks, changing tack.

"That's another thing, why didn't you respond to my questions? You're supposed to reassure the client that the situation is under control."

"Oh, it was under control! I just wanted you to feel immersed in the experience and get the full effect. The intercom reminds you that you're in a blank room with a computer-generated environment."

"I already know full well that it's not real, I've worked here for ten years!" Ellen's fists are clenched as she tries to suppress her mounting frustration.

"OK, I know," he puffs out a little air. "The truth is, I was trying to minimise the amount of stimulation in the room. I thought it would be easier to gauge the integration of two people with fewer variables." His breezy dismissal of Ellen's arguments is growing irritating.

Ellen has evidently reached the threshold of her tolerance. Her voice is holding back emotion, but she manages "I need some air," and walks to the door. I follow her out. The Professor doesn't call after us.

33

The walk to Ellen's house is terse. She is fully immersed in a foul mood, and I am tempted to say I will go back to my place alone. But I want to cheer her up, so I let her work out some of her frustrations in her head as we walk back.

A low level of adrenaline is still trickling through my system; like the buzz you get after riding the biggest rollercoaster. Once the shock of the glitch faded away, I wished we had stayed to try the scenario again. Having another person in the lab gave it a much more realistic feeling, and the idea of joining in with one of Ellen's personal scenarios was enticing. I decide that I will tell her this later when she had cooled down. I can't work out whether it was the patronising way the professor had addressed the situation that was annoying Ellen more than the actual glitch in the multi-user experience.

We arrive at Ellen's house, greeted by a slobbery Ted. Ellen cheers up slightly at his overexcited welcome home.

"If you don't mind, I'd like to head straight out and give Ted a walk - he's been in all day." Without waiting for an answer, she clips a rope lead to Ted's collar. "I'll pick us up some Chinese food whilst I'm out, there's a place I go to regularly just around the corner," she rummages around in a drawer by the front door and hands me a menu. "Just text me what you pick, and I'll get it on the way back."

"Sounds good," I say. My face must not look *good* because she drops Ted's lead and steps in for a hug.

"Sorry I am being moody; I promise I'll cheer up when I've had a walk and some food." She says close to my ear. The rush of her rosy smell and sudden press of contact makes my stomach flip.

"I didn't even notice," I say with a wry smile as she pulls back.

"After you've picked what you want to eat, I'm delegating the task of evening ambience to you," she smiles properly for the first time. "There's wine in the fridge and a stack of vinyl next to the sofa. Guest choice for both," she says as she leads Ted out of the door.

A surge of excitement rises. I nip upstairs to find the loo. There are two other rooms leading off the small corridor. One door is open, showing a dark bedroom with an unmade double bed. I poke my head in and see burgundy bedsheets trailing onto the floor, a small pine bed side table and a matching dresser and wardrobe on the other side of the room. Aside from small bag of toiletries on the table, and a few piles of discarded clothes on the floor, Ellen does not appear to own much.

A fevered curiosity takes over as I regard the other, closed, door. *Ask for a tour!* I tell myself, but then I am depressing the handle and pushing the door open a fraction. Immediately I realise my observation about Ellen's minimalist set up is incorrect. The small room is absolutely rammed with things. Folders, papers and various bits of electronic equipment, none of which resemble anything I have seen before. The volume of random things gives me heart palpitations; the room feels suffocating. I close the door, hearing some papers slide along the carpet trapped under the frame.

This is more than enough snooping, so I go to relieve my bladder in the comparatively empty bathroom. I marvel at her sparse collection of toiletries. One shampoo bottle. One facial wash. A tooth brush and tooth paste. I feel like if I forget to exfoliate and tone my face one day, I'll wake up with sixty-three blackheads. Some people are so lucky.

Back downstairs, I pull a wine out of the fridge at random and twist the cap off. I am secretly pleased that Ellen doesn't have wine that requires a bottle opener as I always manage to split the cork. As I start to pour the wine, I realise I have forgotten to text Ellen my Chinese food order. I pull my phone from my pocket and type a hasty message:

"After much deliberation, I've settled on chow mien please! And prawn crackers if poss x."

Ellen replies immediately "Good choice x."

I fixate on the kiss. Even though this is fairly obviously a date, I still latch on to any signs that things are going as expected. I carry the wine through to the living room and set up on the coffee table. As instructed, I look beside the sofa and there is indeed a stack of vinyl. I spend a long time perusing her eclectic music collection. She has albums spanning several generations and genres, it's hard to narrow down the selection. I decide to go with music I feel will work well in the background, but also set the scene a little. I reluctantly shelve *Led Zeppelin* as inappropriate for the purpose.

Soon, Ellen returns with a bag of food and less-energetic Ted.

"Shall I grab some plates?" I ask as she removes her jacket.

"Nah, that's what the box is for!" she says, the crinkle has reappeared around her eyes. "But a couple of forks would be handy."

She carries the food through to the living room and places it on the coffee table next to the wine.

"Patti Smith! Oh, great choice!" she congratulates my album choice and chimes in singing the chorus to *People have the power*. Seeing her so relaxed and open is invigorating, and when the chorus fades back into to verse I pull her close and kiss her fully on the lips. She reciprocates, and I feel the familiar warmth spreading, but then she pulls away.

"My stomach was rumbling so loud in the queue, it was quite embarrassing." She really does have a knack for diverting a heated situation. We sit on the floor of the living room and devour the Chinese food listening to the music. I punctuate the conversation void with chit-chat, but quickly get the sense than Ellen is content just eating and listening to music. Something I too have grown used to living alone. Half way through the meal she finishes her glass of wine, so fetches the rest of the bottle from the kitchen. When she is gone, I hastily finish my glass too.

When all that remains of dinner is empty cardboard boxes and a plastic bag, we retreat to the sofa. Ellen changes the album over to my next choice Wolf Alice - *My Love Is Cool* stacked beside the player. She lifts her glass to me as the opening beats of *Turn to Dust* drift from the speakers.

"Another great choice," she says sitting back next to me on the sofa, closer than earlier. It crosses my mind to ask her about the situation at the lab, but she seems to have cheered up considerably since then and re-treading the path seems foolish. Instead, I sweep a piece of hair from her cheek and use this as an initiation to lean in and kiss her. This time she allows the situation to develop. I am about to remove Ellen's t-shirt when a loud grumble comes from the other side of the room. I had totally forgotten about Ted.

Ellen laughs. "Yeah, maybe we should take this upstairs, away from this grumpy old man."

My heart quickens. I am actually being invited upstairs. This has more potential than a quick one-sided orgasm.

Taking it upstairs doesn't involve the passionate kissing and sexy wrestling I've seen in films. Instead, we dash upstairs slightly tipsily. Ellen leads me into her bedroom and makes an apology about the mess. I don't bother dismissing the comment and wordlessly remove her t-shirt, enjoying the soft movement her breasts make as she lifts her arms to release the top. I push her back onto the bed and kneel across her legs whilst I remove my own t-shirt and bra. Leaning down close to her face, I let my breasts touch hers, causing a shiver of excitement to run down my spine, then press against her so our torsos are flush, and our lips locked.

We kiss; necks, breasts, bellies, thighs. The sensation of her warm freckled skin against my lips is intoxicating. I press for more and she yields, my fingers curious. Then she rolls onto her stomach and reaches down underneath the bed. I hear latches flipping, then she rummages and returns with a clear dildo suspended from two fabric loops. She hands it to me with an enquiring look, reading my response to the toy.

Recognising this as a strap on, but not knowing exactly how one straps it on, I take a moment to turn the toy over in my hands, trying not to look too confused. Ellen senses my hesitation and says, "Only if you want to?"

In affirmation, I stand, remove my bottoms and step into the two leg holes. As I hoist the dildo up, the adjustable belt starts to make more sense and I catch Ellen looking at me with a twisted smile. She is enjoying watching. The sight of her bare reclined body sets something aflame inside me.

I unbutton her jeans, and firmly tug them down her legs, bringing her knickers with them. She giggles at my sudden forcefulness, and I decide to play along. When her legs are free from the trousers, I grab hold of her hips and roll her over onto her front. The stark nudity of her back is thrilling. Tiny goose pimples rise to the surface of her skins as I caress her. I suddenly have flashbacks to the massage scenario that Ellen had seen me experience. *She* definitely knows what turns women on. I let my hands slide between her thighs; apparently so do I.

Later, we lie entwined and quiet. The music that had drifted from the living room has ceased and I am aware that the next move is coming up. I am almost afraid that she is going to kick me out now, based on previous experience. I hold my breath and think. Then I notice her breathing has changed to the deep, slow sounds of slumber. She has fallen asleep!

I uncurl myself and try to creep out of the room discreetly to the toilet. I make it to the bathroom without turning on any lights and avoid looking at my face in the mirror as I wash my hands. I don't want to remind myself that I was planning to sleep in my makeup, without having brushed my teeth. When I return to the bedroom, Ellen is sitting up in bed.

"Sorry for waking you," I whisper, climbing back into the bed sheepishly.

"Nah you didn't, I was having a weird nightmare about the lab."

"I'm not surprised after the face swap incident!" I level my voice to the normal volume Ellen is using, suddenly wide awake.

"It's not even that, I just don't have a good feeling about this new stage the Professor is planning. Why mess with it?" I realise that she must have been thinking about this a while to want to talk. Or perhaps the growing darkness of the room feels like the right place to release the pressure.

"I guess he's just thinking of science and innovation."

"I am a scientist," Ellen objects. "But I know where the boundaries are when you are messing with people's minds. I'm worried that Eric doesn't. Or he's pushing boundaries he shouldn't."

"Aren't you seeing him again tomorrow?" I ask, yawning as the tiredness creeps back in.

"Yes, he's coming to the Vie Lab in the morning." She replies, more alert than I feel.

"Well why not speak to him about it then. He's probably just not thought it all the way through yet. That's what research teams are for." I wrap my arms around her soft torso, coaxing her to lie back, but she is rigid and unyielding.

34

When I wake up just before 7am the next morning, Ellen is not in the bed. I quickly pull on my jeans and top but am unable to find my bra. Slight panic creeps in when I see that Ellen is also not in the bathroom, or in either of the downstairs rooms. Just when I am about to dial Ellen's number, I hear a key turn in the front door and Ted bursts into the house, bounding past me into the kitchen.

"Morning," Ellen says, stamping her feet on the doormat. "Sorry I left you, had to take Ted out and thought it was best to let you sleep." Ted whines in the kitchen. "He likes his routine; walk at six then breakfast at seven. Has to be exact or he gets fussy," she walks past me into the kitchen, ruffling Ted's black head as he circles her knees.

I stand in the hallway wearing yesterday's clothes, wondering how long I can stay at Ellen's whilst still having enough time to walk home, shower, change and get to work. Not much time at all, I decide. I cross my arms, conscious of the exposed feeling of my braless breasts beneath my t-shirt. Ellen starts preparing Ted's breakfast then opens the fridge.

"I'm not much of a breakfast person," she says looking slightly embarrassed. 'I'm afraid I don't have anything in to offer you."

I bat her apology away, "Oh don't worry, I'll grab something back at my place." This feels like a natural time to leave "I'll just get my stuff together-"

Ellen walks over and pulls me into an embrace.

"It was nice having you stay over for a change," she interrupts. I grin, though she cannot see my face.

"Yeah, thanks for having me," I say, wincing at my overly polite tone. An impatient *bouf* from Ted makes her pull away and back to her task of feeding him.

I nip back upstairs to find my bra and go to the bathroom. When I catch a glimpse of my face, I am mortified to see that my eye makeup has smudged all around my eyes, and my foundation has gone patchy. I regret not washing my face before sleeping, and hurriedly remove the embarrassment with the bar of soap.

Ellen smiles when she sees I have removed my clown make up.

"Looking chipper," she jokes. I cringe. People who don't wear makeup don't understand these things.

She walks with me to the door then there is a pause when I realise I should kiss her. I am conscious that I haven't brushed my teeth, so I keep it brief.

"Let me know how it goes with the Professor," I say as I head towards the gate of her house. She nods and waves, then closes the door. At least there was a gap between the kiss and the door close, feels like progress.

A pleasant contentment rises in me as I walk home in the early morning sunshine.

After getting stuck in a queue at the coffee shop to get a cinnamon raisin bagel and coffee before work, I arrive at my desk just after 9am. Yesterday's tasks seems like a million years ago. The emails dull and automatic. I allow myself 15 minutes to consume my breakfast in peace, then dive into some necessary project admin.

To my surprise, the time flies to lunchtime. I am kicking myself for not preparing food, so I can just work at my desk, when my mobile starts ringing in my bag. I dig it out; it's Ellen.

"Hello," I say cheerful, then hear the choked sounds of crying.

Ellen is out of breath, trying to calm her voice before talking.

"I'm walking to the University," she says between gasps. "Can you meet me somewhere?"

"Sure, erm," I try to think of somewhere quiet to go. "Meet me at the entrance to the park opposite the art gallery? I'll head there now."

Ellen agrees then hangs up. The rumble in my stomach has been supplanted by a queasy feeling.

I dash through the busy streets towards the park. Some people will be taking their lunch outside there, but we'll have a little more privacy than in one of the University cafes.

Ellen is waiting for me at a bench just within the park, her face is blotchy with the remnants of tears. I offer her a hug, but she declines.

"I'll just start crying," she says quietly.

"Did something happen with the Professor?" I ask, hoping hope desperately it's not the end of our relationship instead.

"He's completely lost it," Ellen says, her voice thick. "All those years of building the Vie Lab and now he wants to sell it."

"Sell it!" I exclaim, genuinely shocked "But I thought it was his life's work?"

"Exactly!" she agrees, wiping her nose on a tissue. "But apparently, he's been looking for a potential 'partner', for a while," she uses her fingers to emphasise quotation marks around the word partner, then sadness overcomes her, and she lets out a small sob. "Partner! What have I been for the past ten years? His glamorous assistant? I think that's how he sees it. He said for the project to develop we need input from a larger organisation."

I am dumbstruck, I barely know the guy, but this feels like a kick in the teeth even to me. I reach over to hug her, but she shrugs away.

"That crafty bastard," Ellen spits through her teeth. "Having me do the work whilst he's out making deals behind my back."

"Who is he planning to sell it to?" I ask when she has calmed down slightly.

"A frigging pharmaceutical company!"

"What? For drug testing?" My brain scatters around trying to think of the logic in the decision.

"No, sadly that wouldn't work, or I'd be more enthusiastic. Apparently, they are expanding into the field of biotechnology, trying to stay ahead of the game. And the Vie Lab caught their interest."

"So, he has a buyer lined up?" Ellen nods and pulls out her phone. She shows me the screen she has already loaded, the chrome and white website of INfusion Pharmaceuticals. I take the phone and browse.

"Their key products are manufactured hormones for medicine and research," my voice doesn't mask the worry. "Human growth factor, adrenaline, kisspeptin - what the hell is that?" Ellen shrugs weakly. I make a mental note to research this myself later.

"Eric actually had them draw up a contract over the weekend, he brought it to show me today. They're offering me a job as the head of the research team. Eric just sees it as a lucrative business deal now. I'd love to know how long he's been planning all of this without telling me. But I feel like the truth would be devastating."

"Would you take the job?" I ask, realising as soon as I say it that it's probably not the best time to think about it.

Ellen looks at her feet, twisting her toes into the ground.

"No idea. It feels like I'd be selling out, which would make me a hypocrite. But on the other hand, someone needs to keep an eye on this development in the early stages. How can we let them take full ownership without knowing what they're planning to use it for?"

"So, Eric doesn't know their intention?" I try to keep my voice steady.

"Not from what he said, all he said was they saw it as a great acquisition by the company research and development department, but there are no plans for commercial roll out at present. They are picking up on lots of technological advances. We just happen to be one of them."

"Well, that's kind of good news?" I half ask, grasping at straws for ways to cheer her up.

"Not really," she retorts. "Our plan – Eric and I - was to trial a small scale roll out in the next year or two, once we had secured some funding. But all that is clearly being iced." Mounds of soil collects around the hole she is making with her shoes.

Ellen's phone starts to ring in my hand. I see *Eric* flash on the screen. Ellen makes a noise of frustration and take the phone from me. It seems like she isn't going to answer it, as she glares at the screen for several rings, but finally she does, wordlessly. After a few minutes of listening, her face set with tight lips, she finally utters, "Fine, but Nicole is coming too," she doesn't look to see if I agree to this.

35

Ellen slides her phone back into her pocket and looks up at me, a sadness in her eyes pulls at my emotions.

"I'm not in the right mind set to deal with him," she says, her voice cracking, "but given that he's already racing along with the project sale I want to know what this means for me. Please can you come and be my ears?"

She takes hold of my hand, and we walk out of the park. Before we reach the exit, she drops my hand to adjust her hair, then does not retake it. Given the emotional charge of the day, I don't chance slipping in again. The walk to the lab is quick and quiet. Ellen seems to be deep in thought, and all of my questions feel triggering.

It feels weird to be let in to the storefront of Ryan's bookbinding using a key. Some of the magic is lost without pressing the buzzer. No one is waiting to greet us at reception and Ellen marches straight through to the control room where the professor is sat.

"Ellen, I was worried about you," he says, turning but not rising from the chair. "It's not like you to get emotional."

"What do you expect?!" Ellen exclaims raising her hands "You've basically just dropped a bombshell on my whole life. For the last ten years I have lived and breathed the Vie Suite, you know that." she drops her hands back down. "You are selling out your whole life work, and mine."

"Come on, we always knew this was a potential end point. Right from the start," he says his penetrating gaze unwavering. I am an invisible spectator hovering in the doorway.

"That's not true," Ellen retorts. "At the very beginning you told me you planned to market it to the military for training. But over time things changed and you said that we would exploit the commercial applications of the program *independently*. You never said we would sell it to a third-party company." The sides of Ellen's cheeks and neck look pink and hot.

"I don't think you are seeing the big picture here," the Professor places his fingers together, business man pose. "Working with INfusion will open up so many possibilities. There's only so much we could do as a two-person project you know that."

"Well exactly, which is why we started opening testing to researchers at the University wasn't it? Looking for research projects we could piggyback funding off and expand the research team." Ellen insists.

"There is no money in higher education institutions anymore." The Professor answer calmly, looking at his fingers then back to Ellen. "The best outcomes we could have hoped for in those trials were new avenues of innovation," he pauses, then turns to face me.

"There is fantastic career opportunity for you here too Nicole," he says, a turn of a smile on his mouth, "I have been impressed by what I've seen of you. You seem like a safe pair of hands." I can't place the expression on his face as he says this, a *knowing* look that unsettles me. Before I have chance to question, he continues:

"In any case, how long did you think we would be able to propel the project off the back of expired university funding and my pension?" Ellen opens her mouth then closes it again, not quite ready to argue. "I love the project, dedicated most of my life to it. In fact, I have *lived* most of my life through it." He then swaps to a soothing voice. "Try to think of the positives. This way you're still lead the project, but you'll be able to delegate tasks to other researchers. You might even have time for a life," he smiles but Ellen does not. "I know you feel I should've handed over the project to you but trust me that is too much responsibility for one person. It consumes you. I've spent countless hours worrying about the security of this project and making sure it doesn't get into the wrong hands."

Ellen folds her arms to assert a more solid stance but does not utter a word.

"But at INfusion they have the infrastructure to protect this, to take the protection even further to copyright the software of the code, everything. A dream team of lawyers, a Human Resources department, all you need to do is the research. And I know that's what you want." The Professor seems content with his spiel and leans back to observe Ellen's response.

"So, you're just going to walk away from the Vie Lab after everything you've put into it?" Ellen asks, her voice loosening.

"Of course not, I will be the chair of the steering committee for the whole project. Basically, it means that no major decision can be made without my approval, but I don't have to do anything to do with the day-to-day running. So, I can finally enjoy the retirement I've always dreamed about!" He tries to encourage Ellen to smile with him, but her face is quivering, angrily.

"You'll probably still see me as often anyway, you know what I'm like I just can't stay away."

Ellen doesn't offer any relief to the tension and the room falls silent, then I remember my purpose in the visit.

"So, when exactly are you planning on selling the programme?" I ask, my voice sounds weak and non-committal compared to his.

"Well as off yesterday the sale is final, my lawyer transferred the rights this morning. Hence why I came to the office to discuss with Ellen." He directs the answer to Ellen.

I frown "It's quite late to be telling her this don't you think, how much notice has she got?"

"Technically there is no notice because her job still remains. And it didn't seem sensible to discuss all of the ins and outs with Ellen until I knew it was actually happening. Business deals fall through all the time."

"So, this isn't the first time you've tried?" Ellen asks, her arms sliding back to her side.

"This is the first time anything has taken off, but I've had a couple of leads," he replies, sliding his knuckles under his smooth chin. "I almost went the private investment route via a contact at the University. Sadly, it transpired that he had more inheritance than sense and we didn't see eye-to-eye in the end." He expels air through his lips, fatigue in his face as he recalls the situation.

"How could you have not mentioned this to Ellen after all this time working together?" I feel myself getting hot in the face.

"Can you lower your voice please Nicole. Perhaps you don't know the full story." He seems reluctant to explain, but given that Ellen is standing resolutely, he unfolds his justification for the two of us.

"I know full well that Ellen has wanted to expand the team for a long time, she has been running the whole show herself since my retirement. But we just don't have the resources to employ a full team. Going out to tender would risk the secrecy of the software. I just needed to make sure we could secure constant funding. Working with INfusion is a fantastic opportunity for us all. They are renowned in the pharmaceutical industry, and they're set to be the next big thing in biotechnology. We're coming in at a great time."

His regurgitated business pitch is making me feel sick.

Ellen swallows loudly and says, "What am I supposed to do about my job here?"

The Professor smiles and swings his chair around to face one of the computer screens, bringing up a calendar. "INfusion want us to freeze operations over here until they have established the office space and early-stage support team," he says, facing the screen. "So that gives you about a month of long overdue holiday Ellen. More if you choose to take it.

You're a highly valued member of staff at INfusion now, they'll be flexible on your official start date."

"You're not really giving me much choice about this are you? You've essentially sold me as well as your life's work," Ellen says through trembling lips.

"Not at all, the job acceptance is voluntary," he turns back round to look at her. "And if you don't want to take it, I will pay you a redundancy package."

I can tell Ellen feels trapped by the situation, so I try to buy more time with questions.

"What will happen to the clients here? Are INfusion going to absorb them too?"

"Oh no," he says, with a hint of a laugh. "I cancelled the upcoming client appointments this morning and sent a courtesy email to the mailing list to say the testing period is complete. INfusion don't intend to continue the operation in the same way we have. As I said, it's more of a research operation."

He clasps his hands together, and I get the sense that he is growing tired of justifying his decision to us. "I know they have screened a few people to continue with testing, but there is no intention to roll the programme out publicly as yet."

"Screened how?" I ask, realising this is my own curiosity rather than helping Ellen but at least I am getting him to talk.

"Just background checks, reading over case files, *getting a feel* for the person, that sort of thing." He replies, "Always good to have a trusted pair of hands on the project." His face shifts back into the curious smile, making my skin prickle.

"That sounds like an invasion of privacy," I say, my voice verging on shrill.

"All part of the acquisition process and done in complete confidence I assure you." He sighs the final sentence.

"I should probably get back to work," I say, my thoughts spinning with paranoid anxieties. "Ellen, do you want to come for some fresh air?" she nods.

"Thanks for stopping by Nicole," the Professor says, now swirling his chair back to face the computer. "Please do have a think about a research position at INfusion, I could certainly sort that out."

Ellen follows me back out down the stairs onto the quiet side street.

"Holy shit," I exclaim as soon as we reach the fresh air. "Has he turned into a professional stalker or something? What is he talking about *getting a feel for the person*?"

"I don't know, Nicole, he's just paranoid." Ellen says quietly.

"Wait," a cold panic creeps over my skin, "Are *you* the one who gets a feel for the person?"

"No!" her reply comes as a quick breath, "But, he was probing me for insight about you. Turns out I didn't have much professional intel on you, did I." Her voice fades out. "So that didn't look great."

"Ok so he's probably been digging around for information about me elsewhere?" I try to restrain my voice, but the situation is unsettling me.

"Nicole, I don't know what he's been doing." Ellen says, her voice trembling again, "Clearly, he just does what he likes without telling me anything."

I look at the tears gathering in the corners of her eyes and feel a sudden guilt. "Sorry, yes, I came here to help you. What do you want to do? Go back up and tell him to shove his corporate job up his arse?" I link my arm though hers and squeeze it.

She shakes her head "Maybe he's right."

"What? Have you lost it too? He's selling you *and* his life research project. What about integrity?" I add the last point in an overly twee voice to try and cheer her up, but she does not seem to notice.

"I need to think it all over," she says quietly. My stomach sinks. An hour ago, she was passionately against it, I can't understand how she's been so easily brainwashed by the idea.

"OK well shall we go back to yours?" I ask her. She shakes her head again "No, thanks for coming with me, but you should go back to work. I already feel bad for making you leave."

"No one will even notice I've gone!" I say, a half-truth; it just depends on who decides to stop by my office this afternoon. But she just looks on down the street as though I haven't said anything. I suddenly feel cold all over. I sense that she is retracting away from me.

"OK," I say quietly as we get the end of the main road. "Well in that case, I need to turn off here for the University."

She nods and reaches up for a hug. "Thanks Nicole. I'll text you later."

I walk away from her, desperately trying not to simmer on the situation.

36

The rest of the afternoon is painful. I feel trapped in my office, but I know that going home will not help. I almost ring Riya to chat but realise that going over the whole situation out of context won't make sense. I've only known Ellen for a short time, but I feel so entwined in her life now. I'm worried that she's going to become cold and hard to read again. My thoughts are selfish, but I feel the need for reassurance that Ellen still wants to see me, even without the Vie Lab.

I get back home a little late; the guilt of my extended lunch break encouraging me to stay in the office. My flat feels extra empty, though nothing has changed. I turn my laptop on to an online video channel for background noise then rummage through my sparse kitchen cupboards for something to hash together for dinner.

I almost jump out of my skin when my phone vibrates in my jeans pocket. A message from Ellen:

"I think I'm going to take the job at INfusion. I can't just let it go. At least I'll retain some control there. Ellen."

My heart sinks. Not only because she is copping out of her earlier stance, but she has gone back to impersonal Ellen. I decide to respond neutrally, it's definitely not the time to bring up our relationship, she's clearly got a lot to consider, and I don't want her to make any snap emotional decisions.

"I hope it works out well for you."

Two minutes later my phone rings, it's Ellen.

"That's a bit final," she says as soon as I answer, it sounds like she is crying.

"My text?" I ask perplexed, then re-read it on my phone "I mean I hope everything goes OK at the new job," I tell her.

"Oh, so you're not saying bye to me?" Her voice is so pitiful that my chest goes cold.

"God no, sorry!" Apparently, I am not great at playing it casually cool.

"I'm sorry," Ellen sighs "I'm just a bit all over the place at the moment. The last thing I want is to lose you and my job on the same bloody day." A warm sensation creeps in.

"Understandable," I say, and laugh. She laughs too, then blows her nose.

"Today has been too much," she sighs, "I'm actually just going to go to bed. Feels like a write off."

"Do you want me to come over?" I say without really thinking "I could get us some food on the way over. God knows I haven't got anything to eat here." There's a long pause, then finally she says:

"That'd be great actually. I haven't eaten since this morning so that's probably why I am so irritable."

"Chow mein?" I ask, trying to hide the glee from my voice.

"Gong bao please."

"OK I'll be over ASAP." I hang up the phone to ensure no more misunderstandings happen and quickly search for the Chinese take away near Ellen's house. I place an order whilst putting on my shoes.

Less than half an hour later, I arrive at Ellen's house with a paper bag full of food, marvelling at the speed at which one can obtain a full meal via the internet. Ellen answers the door in light blue button-up pyjamas. I find this endearing, even though it is an indication that she is not feeling well.

She invites me in, and I walk past Ted, lying in the space under the stairs, even his mood seems down. I go into the living room and start to unpack the food packets. Ellen comes in behind me and sits down next to the table.

"I'm glad you're here," she says, "I need a distraction from this shit show."

I laugh "Does that make the Professor the Ringmaster of the *shit show*?"

Ellen actually laughs then stops abruptly. "I must be the dancing bear," she says.

"More like the sad clown," I point to the edge of her downturned mouth. She forces a smile.

I get the impression that Ellen doesn't want to talk about the events of the day any further, so I start to tell her about my work day. The words come out flat and unenthusiastic and I realise that it is not interesting to anyone not involved in the project. So, I quickly change the topic.

"How do you feel about ballet?" I ask her.

She looks up from her food and I see a little flush on her cheeks.

"Honestly," she says, "the only ballet I've seen is what you did in the Vie Lab."

I chuckle at this, "I hope you know that's not actually ballet."

Ellen laughs too, "Yes I assumed as much."

"Well how do you fancy going to a show with me?" I continue.

"What, like an actual public date?" Ellen flashes her wry smile, the one that pulls tiny dimples into her cheeks; it makes my stomach flutter.

"Yes, an actual date. That you have to put nice clothes on for," Ellen does a mock shocked face "We could even double date with my friend Connor and his partner." I continue, testing the water.

"One step at a time!" she says snorting, "I'm not even sure I want to date *you* let alone your whole entourage," my face drops. "I'm just kidding, of course I do!" she leans over and digs me in the ribs.

We dig through our meals in a companionable silence. I realise that for once, Ellen hadn't suggested opening any wine. Whether this is a lack of ceremony or lack of nerves, I can't tell, but there is a comfortable relief to it.

When the food is finished, Ellen sighs deeply "This is going to be a huge change for me," she says, "I've spent most of my adult life devoted to this project. I can't fathom the shift in control."

"It still sounds like you'll have a lot of control over the research," I offer.

"Yeah, I hope so. But presumably I'll be doing a nine-to-five work pattern with evenings to myself."

"You make it sound like that's a bad thing," I exclaim "That's how most people live."

"I know, but it's not as flexible if I have to be in when *they* say." She ruminates for a moment, then continues, "And I suppose, the new-found free time feels weird. I don't even know what you're supposed to do with free time anymore."

This makes me laugh. "That sounds ridiculous, don't be sorry for free time! I'm sure you'll find something to fill it with."

I realise I am being hypocritical as I had the exact same thought when I moved from my PhD to my full-time job. But having friends to spend this time with helped.

"You could start an evening class - pottery is making a comeback," I joke, and she smiles.

"Yeah, or you could teach me how to paint," she laughs.

"Someone needs to teach me first!" And then I remember the painting class I had booked during my week off. It feels good to have something for myself in the diary.

"What about the job offer Eric mentioned to you, would you consider leaving psychology?"

I think for a moment, then shake my head "No, I enjoy my job and I've worked hard to get where I am. As much as I like the Vie Lab programme, I don't think I actually want to work on it full time." I don't say that this is mainly due to the new owners. "But I am definitely happy to help you write scenarios."

I wink, and she says, "Oh so, just the fun bits yeah? Just as well we didn't partner up after all," I know she is just poking fun at me, so I resist the urge to justify my response. I want to maintain her good mood.

Ellen yawns loudly, "Oh god sorry, I've just realised how tired I am. Do you want to get an early night?"

"It's not that early," I say, noting the time.

"Early for me!" she says, gathering the empty boxes into the paper bag for the rubbish.

"Well, you're going to be a nine-to-five woman soon, better get used to it." I realise that I shouldn't have brought the conversation back to this so quickly break into a terrible rendition of Dolly Parton, following her into the kitchen.

"Oh please!" she giggles. "No offence but that voice does not suit you."

I fake being offended. "What voice would suit me?"

"Dusty Springfield?" she offers.

I throw out a few lines from *Son of a Preacher Man* in my best mock-Dusty voice.

Ellen purses her lips and says, "Orr maybe not," and I shoulder barge her.

Now she has perked up, she says, "I've got a present for you," and leads me upstairs. I feel a little worried that she's going to pull out some avant-garde sex toy even though neither of us seem in the mood.

To my surprise, she leads me to the bathroom, and opens the small cupboard under the sink. She reaches in and pulls out a brand-new plastic toothbrush, handing it to me with exaggerated ceremony.

"Sorry I didn't give you a toothbrush to use last night," she says. "I was dead to the world after that sex," she gestures at the handful of toiletries in the room. "And feel free to use anything else you need," she pats me on the hip and leaves the room. I catch my expression in the bathroom mirror, I am visibly over the moon. Is Ellen my girlfriend? I want to ask but feel old-fashioned in my desperation for a label. I brush my teeth and use Ellen's soap to remove my make-up. It makes my face feel tight, but I don't care.

I head to the bedroom and remove my clothes. Slipping under her duvet feels alien to my naked body, even though I was only here last night. The bed smells like Ellen and I enjoy pulling the duvet up around my head to be engulfed in the sweet, slightly rosy scent. Soon, Ellen joins me in the bedroom. She climbs in to the bed and immediately turns to face away from me. I almost feel dejected until she shuffles herself back to press into my front, making herself the little spoon. Her skin is hot against mine, almost too warm. I start to feel aroused by her soft body touching mine, but as I listen to her breathing slow and deepen, I realise that she has fallen asleep. I place my arm over her body on top of the duvet and tuck her closer to me, drifting off to the familiar smell of her skin.

Epilogue

Re: Marketing campaign 001 - prelaunch text for approval

Dear Professor McAllister,

Please find below the INjoy pre-launch copy we discussed on the phone. As noted, this is intended to be a viral marketing campaign - a teaser for the full launch early next year. An image is attached as an example mount for the text:

"Experience everything you have ever dreamt of.

Sooner than you can imagine.

- INjoy"

We're also working on mock-ups for the biological features. R&D are about to test in the human models, so we'll be set to launch soon.

Let me know your thoughts,

Iain Russo

Head of Brand Development
INfusion

ABOUT THE AUTHOR

Alicia V McClane

Alicia lives in the North of England.
She writes at every opportunity.
Neurophysiology and the Human Heart is her first novel.

Printed in Great Britain
by Amazon

32443290R00133